The Secret of the Tibetan Treasure

"It's pure gold," the museum curator said, handing the horse to Nancy.

Nancy took the statue, surprised at how heavy it was. She ran her fingers along the horse's intricate mane, its smooth arched back, and its bridle of rubies. "It's gorgeous," Nancy said.

"A treasure," Nelson Stone remarked as Nancy handed back the Golden Horse. "But so far, it's brought me nothing but trouble. I'll tell you more about that after you read the letter."

Nancy followed Mr. Stone down a corridor and settled into a plush leather chair in his office. The curator pulled a piece of paper from his desk drawer and handed it over. Nancy was just unfolding the letter when Nelson Stone suddenly jumped up from his seat. "I can't remember if I locked that case," he muttered as he headed out the door.

The next moment, Nancy was startled by an anguished cry from the corridor.

"It's gone!" she heard Nelson Stone shout. "The Golden Horse has been s

Nancy Drew
Mystery Stories

Available from MINSTREL Books

108

NANCY DREW®

THE SECRET OF THE TIBETAN TREASURE

CAROLYN KEENE

A MINSTREL® BOOK

PUBLISHED BY POCKET BOOKS

New York   London   Toronto   Sydney   Tokyo   Singapore

A MINSTREL PAPERBACK *ORIGINAL*

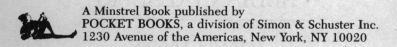

A Minstrel Book published by
POCKET BOOKS, a division of Simon & Schuster Inc.
1230 Avenue of the Americas, New York, NY 10020

Copyright © 1992 by Simon & Schuster Inc.
Produced by Mega-Books of New York, Inc.

ISBN: 0-671-73054-1

First Minstrel Books printing August 1992

10 9 8 7 6 5 4 3 2 1

Cover art by Aleta Jenks

Printed in the U.S.A.

Contents

THE SECRET OF THE
TIBETAN TREASURE

1

An Emergency Phone Call

Nancy Drew dashed down the hall stairs and picked up the telephone on the second ring. "Hi, Bess!" she said cheerfully. Nancy had been expecting her friend, Bess Marvin, to call back to set a time to meet at the mall.

Instead, a strange muffled voice came through the receiver. "This is the Pentagon calling Nancy Drew."

Nancy grinned. "Come on, George Fayne," she said to her other best friend. "I know it's you."

George chuckled. "I guess I shouldn't play around like that," she said. "Someday the Pentagon might really phone the world's greatest detective for help."

Nancy laughed. "And I'll probably hang up on them, thinking it's one of your jokes."

1

"Actually, I was wondering if you were in the mood for a game of tennis," George said.

Just then the operator came on the line. "I have a call for Ms. Nancy Drew," she said. "The caller says it's an emergency."

Nancy bit her lip. "Oh, no!" She'd kept the phone tied up all morning. "I'll be right off," she assured the operator.

"It must be the Pentagon now," George quipped.

"I'll call you back," Nancy promised. She put down the receiver, and the phone rang immediately.

"Nancy Drew speaking," she said, tucking a strand of red-blond hair behind her ears.

"Miss Drew!" a man's voice blurted. "Sorry to break in—but I have an urgent problem. I need to meet with you as soon as possible."

"Can you give me a few details over the phone?" Nancy asked.

"Y-yes, of course," he stammered nervously.

Nancy pulled a pencil and notebook from her purse. "Let's start with your name," she said in a businesslike tone.

The man hesitated, and Nancy wondered whether he was afraid someone was listening in on their conversation.

"My name is Nelson Stone," he said finally, a note of self-importance entering his voice. "I am the curator of the new Clinton Park Museum. A friend gave me your name."

Nancy's mind raced. She recalled her father, Carson Drew, mentioning that the museum was having some kind of legal problem. Nancy's father was a well-respected attorney in River Heights. Then Nancy remembered that a wealthy socialite, Amanda Lane, had donated her mansion to the museum before she died. The papers had been drawn up by Carson, who had been her attorney.

But Amanda's grandniece, Hillary Lane, had been bitter about her aunt's donation. She felt the mansion should have remained in the family, and she was starting a legal battle to contest the donation.

"Does this have anything to do with Hillary Lane?" Nancy asked bluntly. If it did, she knew she would have to consult with her father before taking the case.

"It may," Nelson Stone hedged. "But then again, it may not."

"If you want me to help you," Nancy said firmly, "you'll have to give me specific details."

Mr. Stone sighed. "I've just received a threatening letter. I think someone's out to kill me."

"Where are you right now?" Nancy asked.

The curator cleared his throat. "I'm in my office at the museum."

"I can be there within the hour," Nancy said, glancing at her watch. "But if you really think someone's out to kill you, why don't you contact the police?"

Mr. Stone breathed another deep sigh. "If possible, I'd like to keep the police out of this," he said. "At this point, all I need is a private detective to find out who sent me the letter. Quite frankly, Ms. Drew, I'm in a panic about this. But at the same time, I don't want any bad publicity."

Nancy assured the curator that she would be right over. Hanging up the phone, she wondered why anyone would threaten Nelson Stone. He certainly seemed panicky.

Nancy called George back. "Guess what?" she said. "I may have a new case. Want to drive out to the Clinton Park Museum with me? I have to meet with someone there."

"You've got to be kidding," George said. "It's such a great day for tennis. Can't you put it off for another day?"

"I don't think so," Nancy said. "This guy sounded serious. He thinks someone's out to kill him."

George paused. "I guess that's a good reason for not playing tennis," she said.

"I'd better call Bess," Nancy said. "She thinks we're meeting at the mall."

"Oh, I'm sure my cousin would much rather be at the scene of a murder," George said with a chuckle. She and Nancy both knew how Bess hated to be involved in anything dangerous. "But if you don't call her, she'll probably feel left out."

After hanging up with George, Nancy punched Bess's number into the phone. She knew she was lucky to have the two cousins for friends. They were both loyal and fun, always eager to help Nancy solve a mystery, but they were complete opposites in other ways. Blond and pretty, Bess was a few pounds

4

overweight and was always talking about a new diet. She loved shopping, eating, and thinking about boys. Dark-haired George had a slim, athletic build. Gutsy and practical, she often joined Nancy on dangerous missions.

Bess picked up on the third ring and quickly agreed to join Nancy and George.

Nancy hurried up to her room and slipped a yellow linen blazer over her T-shirt and jeans. Then she ran a comb through her shoulder-length hair, tucked a spiral notebook in her shoulder bag, and rushed downstairs again.

Ten minutes later Nancy had picked up Bess and George in her blue Mustang, and the girls were on their way to the Clinton Park Museum.

A soft breeze blew through the car as Nancy braked for a red light. "Do either of you know anything about a guy named Nelson Stone?" she asked her friends.

"Not much," Bess said from the backseat. "My mother's friend is the real estate agent who rented a house to him here. He's only been in the area about six weeks, since the museum opened."

"And last weekend," George offered, "he was a guest at the club. I was paired with him in a tennis match."

Nancy glanced at George. "So, what did you think of him?"

George ran her fingers through her short dark hair. "Well, he has a great serve," she said, "and an awful backhand."

"Get serious!" Bess told her.

5

"All right," George laughed as the traffic light changed and Nancy drove across the intersection. "To tell you the truth, he seemed kind of stuffy."

"I got the same impression over the phone," Nancy said. Making a right turn, she entered the town of Clinton Park and drove up a steep hill. A few moments later the Clinton Park Museum came into view.

"What a neat place," Bess gushed, gazing wide-eyed at the majestic mansion. It was surrounded by large formal gardens and neatly clipped hedges.

"It sure is," George agreed.

Now Nancy could understand why Hillary Lane was so bitter that her aunt donated the mansion. Hillary had probably had a sentimental attachment to the gorgeous building. Nancy drove slowly through the front gate and followed a long gravel driveway to the parking lot. Finally she pulled into a space, and the girls scrambled out.

Nancy tucked her keys into her purse and took out the spiral notebook. Her mind was now fully focused on meeting Nelson Stone.

"I know that look in your eyes," George teased as the three of them hurried toward the museum. "You're ready to start a new case."

Nancy grinned. "The beginning is easy," she said. "The problems come later."

"Oh, no!" Bess cried suddenly. A sign in front of them read: The Clinton Park Museum Is Closed for School Tour.

"So much for seeing the museum," George said,

6

sighing. "I guess we'll have to wait for you outside, Nancy."

"At least there's a refreshment stand," Bess said brightly. She pointed to a striped awning near the front entrance where a group of school children were gathered. "It looks as if it's open."

George rolled her dark eyes. "I thought you were on a new diet."

"Oh, I am," Bess replied, flashing a naughty grin. "It's called the junk-food diet. I'm going to get some ice cream," she added. "Catch up with you later."

Crossing the manicured grounds with George, Nancy was aware of the fragrance of fresh-cut grass. The chopping sound of garden clippers filled the air as they passed a man shaping a tall hedge.

"Wow!" George explained. "Take a look at that mermaid."

Nancy turned and glanced at the smiling gardener, thinking her friend was joking. Then she realized that the gardener was shaping the hedge into the graceful form of a mermaid. "That's really beautiful," she told him. He nodded pleasantly.

George admired the sculptured hedge from another angle. "I wonder how he did that," she said.

"Listen," Nancy said, glancing at her watch, "I'd better get a move on. I'll meet you out here after I talk with Mr. Stone, okay?"

A few minutes later Nancy was inside the cool marble halls of the museum. A silver-haired security guard sat behind a desk in the hallway. The name tag on his lapel read Ralph Hayes. He told Nancy that the museum was closed for a special school tour, but Nancy quickly explained that she had an appointment with Nelson Stone.

The security guard studied her with watery blue eyes. "Oh, right," he said. "You must be Ms. Drew. Just sign your name in the visitors' book." He pushed a large leather-bound book across the desk and handed her a ball-point pen.

As Nancy scribbled in her name, she was surprised to see Hillary Lane's name on the line above.

When she looked up, she saw a dignified-looking man, dressed in a navy blue suit, walking toward her. For a moment she studied the short, well-groomed figure. Everything about him was neat and precise.

That's got to be Stone, Nancy thought, moving toward him. "Mr. Stone?" she asked.

"Yes," he replied in the same refined, nervous voice she had heard earlier on the phone. "May I help you?" Then he raised a thick eyebrow. "Just a moment," he said. *"You're* Nancy Drew? I thought you'd be . . ."

"Older," Nancy finished, with a smile. At eighteen, she had grown accustomed to such comments.

The curator shrugged. "I suppose age is not important. Anyway, you seem to have an excellent reputation as a detective. I understand you've solved a number of cases."

"A fair number," Nancy replied, looking squarely into Nelson Stone's deep-set brown eyes.

"Very well then," he said, guiding Nancy past a

display of Babylonian vases. Nearby, a teacher was leading a tour of chattering schoolchildren. "Let's go to my office," Mr. Stone said. "I'll show you the letter."

Nancy followed the curator into the Egyptian section, which was lined with huge bronze statues of Egyptian pharaohs. "The museum certainly has an interesting collection," Nancy remarked as they passed a glass case filled with ancient Egyptian jewelry.

"Most of these artifacts are on loan from other museums," Mr. Stone explained. "Though we are very proud of our permanent collection," he added quickly as they passed under a marble archway into the next room. "Especially our most recent acquisition, the Golden Horse."

A shaft of sunlight streamed through the stained-glass window as they entered the Tibetan section, a small room filled with Buddhist artifacts. Nancy's eyes were immediately drawn to a small golden statue of a horse, displayed in a glass case in the center of the room.

"It's magnificent!" Nancy stepped forward to admire the Golden Horse. The statue was no more than twelve inches high, made from the same burnished gold as the other artifacts in the room. With its prancing stance, the horse looked as if it were about to jump out of the case.

"It's also very valuable," Nelson Stone told her. "The museum has just bought it for a little over a million dollars."

9

"It must be very old," Nancy commented.

"Indeed it is," the curator said, stooping down to the floor panel beneath the case.

Nancy watched as he slid back a false panel and flicked a switch.

"I'll just deactivate the burglar alarm system before I open the case," Mr. Stone said. He rose and took a key from his jacket pocket. Then he unlocked the glass case and carefully removed the Golden Horse.

"It's pure gold," he said, handing the horse to Nancy.

Nancy took the statue, surprised at how heavy it was. She ran her fingers along the horse's intricate mane, its smooth arched back, and its bridle of rubies. The horse's flowing tail was carved in minute detail, and every straining muscle was clearly defined. "It's gorgeous," Nancy said.

"A treasure," Mr. Stone remarked as Nancy handed back the Golden Horse. "But so far it's brought me nothing but trouble."

"Why do you say that?" Nancy asked as the curator returned the artifact to the case.

"I'm afraid I stepped on a few toes when I purchased it for the museum," he replied, leading Nancy down the corridor. "I outbid some people who wanted it for their own private collections. And then the museum trustees frowned on my spending so much on one piece. But I'll tell you more about that after you read the letter."

Turning left, Mr. Stone led Nancy past a partly open

office door. As she glanced in, Nancy noticed a red purse lying on a chair.

"This way, Ms. Drew," Nelson Stone said as they reached his office. He closed the door and sat down behind his desk. "Please have a seat."

Nancy settled into a plush leather chair and looked over the many artifacts Stone had displayed in his office. The curator pulled a piece of paper from his desk drawer and handed it over. Nancy was just unfolding the letter when Nelson Stone suddenly jumped up from his seat.

"I can't remember if I locked that case," he muttered over his shoulder as he headed out the door.

Nancy skimmed the contents of the letter the curator had given her. It was typed on thick bond paper, and the letters were very faint. The sender hadn't bothered to put in a fresh typewriter ribbon, Nancy thought.

The next moment Nancy was startled by an anguished cry from the corridor.

"It's gone!" she heard Nelson Stone shout. "The Golden Horse has been stolen!"

2

A Fruitless Search

Nancy dropped the letter on the desk and grabbed her bag. Then she ran out of the curator's office and bolted down the corridor to the Tibetan section. There, in the center of the room, Nelson Stone stood, shaking his head at the empty case. Turning to Nancy, he cried again, "It's gone! I can't believe it!"

Mr. Stone's eyes looked vacant. Realizing he was in shock, Nancy took the curator by the arm and guided him gently back to his office. "Did you see anyone?" she asked, hurrying him down the corridor. She was eager to phone the police as soon as possible.

"I just can't believe it would disappear like that," Mr. Stone mumbled. "We were only away for a few minutes."

"It didn't just disappear," Nancy said grimly. "Someone obviously took it."

The curator sank into the leather chair in his office with a dazed look. "This is a nightmare," he moaned.

"I'll be right back," Nancy said quickly. She left Nelson Stone's office and rushed to the security guard near the front entrance of the museum. When she saw that he was dozing, she sighed, feeling frustrated. She figured it was useless to wake him up. The guard had probably been asleep since she left him. She could talk to him later.

Nancy headed back to Stone's office. She reached for the phone and started to put a call through to the Clinton Park police.

Nelson Stone buried his face in his hands and shuddered. "Please don't call the police. Think of all the publicity. This will ruin me. I can't face the police right now. Can we wait awhile?"

Nancy put down the receiver. "I know you're upset, Mr. Stone, but there's a chance the police will find the Golden Horse," she said. "The faster we move on this, the better."

"Will we have to tell them I left the case unlocked?" the curator asked, wringing his hands. "The Museum Society could have me fired."

"We'll have to tell the police the truth," Nancy said. "I'm sorry, but we have no choice."

Despite Stone's pleading, Nancy finally put a call through to the police. She answered a few initial questions and was told that a police car was on its way.

After hanging up, she did her best to console the curator, who still seemed totally distraught.

A few minutes later Nancy hurried out the front door and ran down the wide steps of the museum. Her friends were talking to the gardener and a young woman by the hedge. "George! Bess!" Nancy called. "Come quick!"

George sprinted toward Nancy, with Bess just behind her. "What's up?" George asked.

Nancy filled her friends in on the situation. "The museum's most valuable piece has just been stolen."

At that moment the gardener approached with the young woman. He introduced himself to Nancy as Lee Tung and said his daughter's name was Su-Lin.

"Did you say something's been stolen from the museum?" Su-Lin asked, pushing back a lock of glossy jet-black hair. Su-Lin appeared to be about twenty years old. She was attractively dressed in black leggings, a long pink shirt, and a lavender brocade vest. A strand of amethyst beads hung from her neck.

"It just happened," Nancy explained. "Someone stole the Golden Horse."

The gardener and his daughter gasped.

"Did any of you see anyone leave the building?" Nancy asked.

They all stared blankly at her.

"No," Bess replied. "We were watching Mr. Tung shape the hedge, but I don't think anyone went by."

"Wait a minute," George said, frowning. "A car drove off a few minutes ago."

"What kind of car?" Nancy asked quickly.

14

George bit her lip. "I can't remember. I didn't pay much attention to it."

"I didn't see any car," Bess said with a shrug. "Sorry."

The gardener shook his head sadly. "What a shame."

"This is terrible!" Su-Lin blurted. "The Golden Horse is the museum's greatest treasure. It's irreplaceable. Are the police on their way?"

As she spoke a siren sounded, and everyone looked toward the gate. A police car was just entering the grounds, swerving past the bus filled with schoolchildren on its way out.

Nancy ran over to the car as it pulled to a halt at the museum's front entrance and two policemen got out. She quickly introduced herself and explained that she was the person who had phoned.

"I'm Lieutenant Higgins," said the taller officer. He had thinning gray hair and piercing blue eyes magnified by thick, rimless glasses. "And this is Officer Jenkins," he added with a nod toward the younger officer as they mounted the front steps of the museum. Entering the building, Lieutenant Higgins asked Nancy, "Isn't there a security guy here?"

Nancy pointed across the hallway to the silver-haired security guard slumped across the desk. In the quiet hallway they could hear his gentle snores.

"Get a load of that," Officer Jenkins remarked.

Lieutenant Higgins strode over to the sleeping guard and shook him gruffly. "Wake up, old-timer," he said.

15

The guard sat up and blinked. "What, what? The museum is closed," he muttered.

"There's been a robbery," Lieutenant Higgins told him. "Did you see anyone leave the building?"

The security guard rubbed the sleep from his eyes and fumbled for the visitors' book.

The lieutenant waved his hand. "Forget it," he snapped. "You won't find the crook's name in there." He turned to Nancy and asked her to take them to the curator's office.

As they passed the Tibetan section, Nancy pointed out the empty display case. "That's where the Golden Horse was kept."

"And where were you at the time of the robbery?" Higgins asked Nancy.

"With Mr. Stone, in his office," she explained as the officers moved over to the display case and inspected it closely.

"Hey, look," Officer Jenkins said. "The glass isn't even broken."

"I can explain that," Nancy said slowly. "Mr. Stone had just unlocked the case to show me the artifact. But then he got distracted. I guess he forgot to lock the case and reactivate the burglar alarm."

The officers exchanged glances.

Officer Jenkins shook his head. "It's amazing how careless some people can be."

Nancy led the officers to Nelson Stone's office, where they found the curator pacing the floor. Nancy was about to take a seat when the lieutenant asked her to leave. He obviously wanted to question Stone alone.

Nancy took a quick tour of the ground floor. She soon discovered that both the back and side entrances to the museum were closed off due to building alterations. Sheets of plywood had been nailed across the doors with large notices reading Exit Closed During Renovation.

Nancy realized that the only exit on the ground floor was through the front entrance. That was odd, she thought. All public buildings were required to have more than one exit on each floor in case of fire.

Obviously, Nancy realized, Nelson Stone was careless about fire safety precautions. And it was that same kind of carelessness with security that was causing him so much trouble now.

Nancy made her way up the wide marble staircase to the second floor. As she passed a gallery of Indian miniature paintings, she suddenly felt a draft in the hallway.

Following the flow of cool air, she came to an open window. Nancy lifted the window higher and looked out. A fire escape led down to the rear courtyard, where a jumbled mass of building equipment and materials lay on the ground.

The mess probably belongs to the renovators, Nancy told herself, but she didn't see any workers around. Leaning farther out the window, Nancy saw the parking lot at the corner of the building.

Someone could have easily gotten out this way, she

reasoned. But then, with the security guard asleep, someone could just as easily have walked out the front door. Unlikely, Nancy decided. No one could absolutely depend on his sleeping.

Nancy ducked back in and closed the window. Then, glancing down, she noticed a shiny object on the floor. Nancy took a closer look. It was a woman's gold earring. She picked it up and tucked it in her pocket, thinking it might be a clue.

During the next few minutes, Nancy roamed through the large empty bedrooms on the second floor, finding nothing more of interest. Some of the rooms had fireplaces. A few of the rooms at the far end of the building were covered with a thick layer of dust. Apparently, the renovators hadn't reached that far yet.

The building was probably too old to have built-in closets, Nancy mused, wondering if the culprit could be hiding in the building. Finding the stairway to the third floor, she saw that it was blocked off with more pieces of plywood. A sign taped to the banister read No Entry.

Nancy thought about removing the nailed plywood and investigating the third floor. But right now she was more eager to see what progress the police were making. As she headed down the stairs to the ground floor, Nancy heard the buzz of children's voices. Another school tour was obviously in progress. Then, passing the Tibetan section on her way to Nelson Stone's office, Nancy noticed Officer Jenkins talking to Su-Lin.

"I just can't believe it's gone," Nancy overheard Su-Lin telling the officer. "The Golden Horse is part of my heritage. You see, I'm half Tibetan," she explained. "That particular statue has a special meaning for me."

Officer Jenkins scribbled in his notebook for another moment, then excused himself to speak with the teacher.

Nancy approached Su-Lin. "I guess you visit the museum often," Nancy said.

Su-Lin forced a smile. "I work here as an intern on weekends," she said. "The internship is part of the anthropology program at Westmoor University."

"Sounds interesting," Nancy remarked. "What sort of work do you do here?"

"Oh, all sorts of things," Su-Lin said. "Sometimes I give guided tours. Sometimes I update catalogs. There's always work to be done in the reference library." With a frown she added, "And, of course, Margaret Parker never stops asking me to do her paperwork."

"So you're overworked and underpaid?" Nancy quipped.

"Something like that," Su-Lin replied. A twinkle appeared in her almond-shaped eyes. "Please don't tell Margaret I said that."

"Don't worry," Nancy assured her. "I don't even know Margaret Parker. Who is she, anyway?"

"Margaret is the assistant curator," Su-Lin said, brushing back her bangs.

"Where's her office?" Nancy asked, thinking it

might be a good idea to speak to the assistant curator herself.

"Margaret's office is down the corridor," Su-Lin replied, pointing behind her. "Just before you get to Mr. Stone's office. But this is Margaret's day off, I think."

Nancy excused herself and hurried down the corridor, toward the assistant curator's office. She remembered seeing a red purse in there before the robbery. Did it belong to Margaret Parker? Nancy wondered if someone else had been in Margaret's office at the time of the robbery.

After turning the corner, Nancy found the assistant curator's door closed. "Hello?" she said, knocking. A moment passed and she knocked again. "Is anyone in?" she called. Still no answer. Nancy slowly turned the knob and opened the door.

Immediately Nancy glanced at the chair, but the red purse was gone. Nancy made a mental note to find out who it belonged to.

Looking around the small cluttered office, a framed photograph on a shelf caught Nancy's eye. It was a portrait of a young blond woman, dressed in a graduation cap and gown. "Probably Margaret Parker," Nancy muttered to herself. Leaning closer, she saw that it was dated five years ago.

After closing the office door behind her, Nancy returned to the corridor, stepped over to Stone's office, and knocked twice.

"Come in," Nelson Stone called.

Nancy entered the room and saw Lieutenant Higgins sitting in a leather chair, scribbling in his note-book. A haggard-looking Nelson Stone was seated behind his desk. It seemed as if the curator had aged ten years.

"Nancy, this is Lieutenant Higgins," Stone said.

The officer looked up from his notebook. "Yes, we've met," he said briskly, returning his attention to his notes.

"Excuse me for interrupting," Nancy said. "I just wanted to ask Mr. Stone where I could find his assistant, Margaret Parker."

"She's off today," the curator said.

Nancy frowned. "But I saw a purse in her office just a little while ago. I'm sure of it."

The lieutenant looked at Nelson Stone and raised his eyebrows.

"The door was partly open when I passed by the office with you this morning," Nancy continued.

The curator shrugged. "What can I say?" he muttered. "I don't know anything about any purse. Margaret is not here today."

Suddenly Nancy heard raised voices outside the door. A moment later the door swung open and all eyes turned to a glamorous blond woman standing before them. She was stylishly dressed in a short, white linen dress and sparkling gold jewelry, which set off her deep tan.

Immediately Nancy recognized Hillary Lane, the beautiful heiress whose great-aunt had donated the family mansion that now housed the museum. Nancy remembered that Hillary had spent several years in

21

Hollywood, where she had starred in quite a few films. But after her great-aunt died, Hillary had given up her acting career and returned to Clinton Park, devoting time to her vast art collection and community activities.

"Lieutenant," Officer Jenkins began, "I found this woman hiding in the library."

"I told you," Hillary said indignantly, "I wasn't *hiding*. I was doing important research for a lecture I'm giving on Oriental art."

Nelson Stone rose from his chair. "Hillary, you know the museum is only open today for employees and school tours," he said.

Hillary's features suddenly hardened. "I didn't think those rules applied to *me*," she replied, tossing back her shiny platinum hair. Then, noticing Nancy, her face brightened. "Why, hello," she said breezily. "You're Nancy Drew, aren't you? I know your father."

Nancy smiled and gave a little wave. She was about to speak when Lieutenant Higgins rose from his seat. "We're dealing with a very serious matter here, Miss Lane," he began. "A valuable artifact has just been stolen."

Nelson Stone stared at his alligator loafers. Nancy sensed the curator's embarrassment as Lieutenant Higgins filled Hillary Lane in on the details.

For a long moment the heiress was speechless. Her expression gave no indication of what she was thinking. Finally she closed her eyes and uttered a pained sigh. "I thought I heard screaming when I was working in the library," she said to Lieutenant Higgins.

"But I imagined it was just another one of Mr. Stone's emotional outbursts with his staff."

Nelson Stone stood up. "How I run the museum is none of your business."

Hillary rolled her eyes. "He should never have been made curator, in my opinion," the heiress said to Higgins in a stage whisper. She turned to Stone and shot him a withering look.

Nelson Stone bristled and seemed about to make a retort when Lieutenant Higgins cut him short. "Okay, okay. You two can continue your private feud later," the officer said. "You can go now, Miss Lane—but we'll probably want to talk with you again."

After Hillary Lane left Mr. Stone's office, Nancy told Lieutenant Higgins why she had originally come to the museum. "Somebody sent Mr. Stone a threatening letter, and he phoned me this morning to start an investigation." Nancy knew that Mr. Stone had wanted to hold back this information, but she thought it best to give the police as much help as possible. There was always a chance that the threatening letter could somehow be connected with the robbery.

Lieutenant Higgins flashed Mr. Stone an annoyed look, and the curator's face reddened with embarrassment. "Why didn't you call the police?" the officer asked him impatiently. "You'd better let me take a look at that letter," he added, holding out his hand.

Mr. Stone handed over the letter. "I didn't think it had anything to do with the robbery," he mumbled.

"I'll be the judge of that," Lieutenant Higgins said firmly. He skimmed the letter and shook his head.

"This is ridiculous," he said finally. "Someone says he wants to kill you because he doesn't like the way you run the museum." The officer folded the letter and tucked it in his pocket. "Sounds like someone has quite a grudge against you. We'll look into it."

"It's all right for *you* to take that letter so lightly," Mr. Stone said. "I'm the one who's been threatened."

Lieutenant Higgins snapped his notebook closed. "I've seen plenty of letters like this in my time," he said. "But they very seldom amount to anything." Then, moving toward the door, he added, "We'll be in touch soon, Mr. Stone." He nodded to Nancy and left.

Nancy turned to Mr. Stone. "I'm sorry I brought up the letter, but I had to tell the truth about why I was here. Besides, there may be a connection between the letter and the robbery."

"I understand," Mr. Stone replied with a sigh. "But do you see what I'm up against? I knew the police wouldn't take that letter seriously. I'm really very frightened."

"I know," Nancy said. "Who do *you* think wrote it?"

Nelson frowned. "I just don't know. It could have been anyone."

"Well, for starters, Hillary Lane doesn't seem to be a big fan of yours," Nancy pointed out.

"No, she certainly isn't," Mr. Stone said darkly.

Nancy thought for a moment. "Where is the reference library?" she asked. "I didn't see it when I was walking around the building."

24

"It's just down the hall," Mr. Stone said with a wave of his hand. "Turn right when you leave my office."

Nancy said goodbye to the curator and promised to speak with him soon. On her way out of the museum she checked out the library, but she found nothing more than a musty room lined with old books. Nancy noted that there was no exit to the outside from the stuffy library.

When Nancy joined George and Bess back at her car, her friends were eager to hear all the details. She was in the middle of telling them what had happened when she saw Nelson Stone leave the museum and walk quickly toward his vintage Cadillac.

Bess sipped her milk shake. "So, go on. What happened when Hillary Lane came in?"

Nancy was about to reply when she heard the sound of skidding wheels. She turned just in time to see Stone's car spin out of control, across the driveway. The car flattened the rose bed and roared across the lawn. Finally it plowed into a line of privet hedges and came to a stop.

Nancy and her friends bolted across the parking lot. As they drew closer to Nelson Stone's Cadillac, Nancy saw the curator slumped over the steering wheel.

3

Compromising Positions

"Mr. Stone!" Nancy called urgently, tugging open the car door. "Are you okay?"

Slowly the curator lifted his head from the steering wheel. "I think so," he said, pressing his fingers to the reddening bruise on his forehead.

Nancy leaned forward and took hold of his arm. "Easy does it," she said, helping the groggy man out of the car.

"What happened?" George asked.

"The brakes failed," Mr. Stone said, still holding his head. "I put my foot down, but nothing happened. I couldn't stop the car."

"You're lucky you weren't going down a steep hill,"

Bess told him. Then she glanced sadly at the demolished mermaid hedge.

Mr. Stone buried his face in his hands. "Someone's out to kill me, I know it!"

"I'll drive you home," Nancy offered. "Unless you feel you need to see a doctor," she added quickly.

Nelson Stone stretched his neck, as if checking for whiplash. "I think the only thing I'm suffering from right now is nerves. I just need to go home and rest."

Nancy turned to Bess. "Would you mind helping Mr. Stone over to my car?" she asked. "I want to check out the Cadillac."

As Bess guided the curator toward the parking lot, Nancy moved around to the front of Mr. Stone's car. Pushing past the flattened hedge, she asked George to get in the driver's seat and pull the release lever on the hood.

The moment Nancy looked under the hood, she could see a dark oil stain running down below the engine. "Push the brake pedal," she called to George.

The next instant Nancy saw a trickle of brake fluid oozing from a rupture in the metal hydraulic brake pipe.

"Do you think that was done on purpose?" George asked.

"Maybe," Nancy said, frowning. "But there's a slim chance that it was a natural break. I'd need an expert's opinion to know for sure."

Just then Lee Tung ran across the front lawn to help the girls push the Cadillac back to the parking lot. "I just heard the commotion from the toolshed," he explained.

After the Cadillac was moved, George and Nancy joined Bess and Nelson in the Mustang. "This day has been a disaster," Nelson Stone grumbled as Nancy drove past the front gate. "First there was the threatening note. Then the Golden Horse was stolen. And now someone has really tried to *kill* me." He shuddered.

"Maybe it was an accident," Bess said. She was sitting beside the curator in the backseat.

Nancy signaled to George not to mention the possibility that the brake pipe had been tampered with. She didn't want to frighten Mr. Stone any more than necessary. But she made a mental note to get a professional opinion on the brake pipe as soon as possible.

Nelson Stone lived in a small ranch-style house on the outskirts of Clinton Park. As they drove up, he leaned forward and said, "Would you girls like to come in for a few minutes?" When Nancy hesitated, Mr. Stone added, "Frankly, Nancy, I'd like you to check out my house."

"All right," Nancy said.

As they walked to Mr. Stone's front door, Nancy wondered how much more tension the man could take. The curator looked pale and drawn, and he was shivering slightly, as if he'd been gripped by a fever.

He fumbled with his keys for a moment, then noticed a package in the letter box. He hesitated before reaching for it.

Nancy saw his hand tremble and took hold of the package herself.

"Maybe it's a nice surprise this time," Bess suggested as they entered the house.

"Hmm," Nancy said, frowning. "No return address." Inspecting the box more closely, she noticed that the brown paper wrapping was torn along one edge, revealing a striped black and gold box underneath.

Bess looked over Nancy's shoulder. "Wow!" she exclaimed. "Gold Flag chocolates."

Nancy unwrapped the package, then smiled. "Bess can detect Gold Flag chocolates from a mile away."

"Actually," Bess confessed as Mr. Stone ushered them into the living room, "I'm on a diet right now. But what harm would one little chocolate do?"

George gave Bess a disapproving look, followed by a quick jab in the ribs. As they sat down on the couch, Bess glared back at George.

"Funny," Nancy said, handing the chocolates over to Mr. Stone. "There's no card inside."

"I can't imagine who they're from," he muttered, tucking the box into a cabinet drawer.

Nancy noticed the disappointed look on Bess's face. Generosity obviously wasn't one of Nelson Stone's strong points.

It took Nancy about fifteen minutes to survey the house. Carefully she checked that all the windows and doors were properly locked and that there was no one hiding in any of the closets.

"Everything looks all right to me," Nancy said

cheerfully as she rejoined the others in the living room. "I guess I don't have to remind you not to let anyone in, Mr. Stone. I'd also suggest keeping the curtains closed and staying away from the windows. We'll talk tomorrow. But meanwhile, if you have any problems, you can call me at home."

Nelson Stone walked the girls to the door. "Thanks for your help, Ms. Drew," he said. "I'm very grateful."

That evening, after Nancy had set the dinner table, she called her father in from his study. "Hannah made fresh onion soup and pot roast for dinner," she said as they sat down at the dining room table.

"Mmm, smells good," Carson Drew said, sniffing the air appreciatively. He opened a linen napkin and spread it across his lap. "Hannah's homemade onion soup is one of my favorites."

A few moments later the housekeeper entered with two steaming bowls of onion soup, topped with crusts of melted cheese. "Careful, they're hot," she warned, placing the bowls on the table. "Go ahead and start. I'll join you in a minute."

"Looks great," Nancy and her father said together. They always appreciated Hannah Gruen's loving attention. She had been with the Drews since Nancy's mother had died when Nancy was three, and they considered her part of the family.

Carson Drew smiled at his daughter. "So, it sounds as if you've had yourself a busy day. Tell me more about this robbery at the museum. Do the police have any suspects yet?"

Nancy took a sip of onion soup. "If they do, I don't think Lieutenant Higgins will be confiding in me. I got the idea he thought Nelson Stone was crazy to hire a teenage detective."

Carson shrugged. "I would have thought your reputation for success had spread to the Clinton Park police by now. It's only the next town over. Chief McGinnis has nothing but good things to say about your work here in River Heights."

"Well, right now I'm more concerned with Nelson Stone," Nancy said. "Especially if that brake pipe was severed by someone on purpose."

"Any leads on who might have done that?" Nancy's father asked.

Nancy broke off a piece of crusty bread and buttered it thoughtfully. "Mr. Stone may have a collection of enemies. At this point, I don't know who'd be vicious enough to try and hurt him. But right now I'd say that Hillary Lane is a prime suspect."

"Hillary Lane certainly isn't fond of Nelson Stone."

"Can you fill me in on the details?" Nancy asked.

"Well, it's a long story," Carson said. "You see, when Hillary Lane gave up her Hollywood career, she expected to be made curator of the Clinton Park Museum, especially since the mansion was donated by her great-aunt. There was some debate among the museum trustees as to whether she had the necessary qualifications, I believe. Hillary has been a big art collector for years, and she has an advanced degree in art history. In fact, I understand she's written some important articles on the subject of Oriental art. But then, so has Nelson Stone, of course. I read in the paper that he was a curator of a museum back East. From bits of gossip I've heard, he used his connections to get the job out here."

"That's very interesting," Nancy said. It sounded as if Hillary Lane had been confident that she'd have another starring role as curator of the Clinton Park Museum. But, Nancy told herself, it was hard to imagine that she'd threaten to kill for it.

At that moment Hannah returned to the dining room with plates of tossed salad and sat down at the table. "I never stop hearing about Hillary Lane these days," the housekeeper muttered. "Ever since she got turned down for that curator's job, she's been as busy as a bee. I just read in the paper that she's organizing this year's dog show for the Clinton Park Humane Society. You can bet your boots it will be a class act, if Hillary Lane is running things."

Carson Drew nodded. "I believe they're holding the event this Saturday on the grounds of her house."

Nancy poked at her salad. Maybe the dog show would be a good excuse to speak with Hillary Lane. She couldn't help wondering if the heiress had slipped out of the library, past Stone's closed office door, and into the Tibetan room, where she'd snatched the Golden Horse. Maybe she'd even done it to embarrass the curator. If that was the case, she'd definitely succeeded. And, of course, if Stone ended up being fired, Hillary had another chance at the job.

After dinner Nancy went upstairs and phoned Nelson Stone. "I thought I'd check in with you," she said. "How's it going?"

"I'm a bundle of nerves," he told her. "But I managed to phone Rapid Repair to have my car towed in. They work around the clock, so maybe I'll have it back by tomorrow."

"Well, that's good," Nancy said. Then she reminded him, "Don't forget to keep your doors locked and take those other precautions I told you about."

After saying goodbye to Mr. Stone, Nancy phoned Clinton Park Information for Hillary Lane's number. She punched the number in, and someone answered on the second ring.

"The Lane residence," a young woman's voice said.

"May I speak with Ms. Lane, please?" Nancy asked, wrapping the telephone cord around her index finger.

"I'm sorry," the woman replied. "Ms. Lane is dining at the moment. May I take a message?"

"This is Nancy Drew—Carson Drew's daughter," Nancy explained. "I was wondering whether I could stop by tomorrow to buy a ticket for the dog show."

The woman hesitated. "Well, I don't know. I believe the tickets will be sold at the gate on Saturday."

"I'll be in the neighborhood tomorrow morning," Nancy pressed. "I could stop by, if you don't mind."

The woman hesitated again. "Well, I guess that would be all right," she said slowly. "If Ms. Lane knows you, I mean."

After hanging up, Nancy sat down on the edge of her bed and gazed out the window at the thin crescent moon rising above the treetops. She couldn't stop thinking about Nelson Stone's brake pipe. Had it been cut on purpose? Without an expert's opinion, she didn't want to jump to conclusions. She decided to pay a visit to Rapid Repair.

Twenty minutes later Nancy was behind the wheel of her blue Mustang. Driving through the streets of River Heights, she turned on the car radio and caught the end of her favorite song. She was still humming when the eight o'clock news came on.

In a matter-of-fact tone the newscaster reported that a precious Tibetan artifact, the Golden Horse, had been stolen from the Clinton Park Museum earlier that day. "The police have stated," the newscaster continued, "that they have no suspects at the present time."

Nancy flashed back to Hillary Lane in Nelson Stone's office. The former actress had seemed so self-assured, as if she owned the place. Her dazzling beauty and self-confidence would probably intimidate most people. Even the hardened Lieutenant Higgins might not consider her a possible suspect.

Nancy drove a few more miles into Clinton Park, then slowed down. She wasn't planning to stop, but she wanted to get a good look at Nelson Stone's house as she passed.

The house was in darkness, except for the yellow porch light, which cast shadows on the front lawn. Nancy's eyes searched each patch of darkness. Then, certain there was no one lurking around the bushes, she pressed down gently on the accelerator and headed toward downtown Clinton Park.

A few minutes later she saw a neon sign that read Rapid Repair—Open 24 Hours.

Nancy drove into the station and parked her car beyond the gas pumps. A single fluorescent light illuminated the office. Opening the door, she heard a country western song playing on the radio.

"Can I help you, miss?" asked a bearded man in blue overalls. He slid a booted foot off the desk and removed an unlit cigar from his mouth.

"I understand you towed Nelson Stone's car in for repair," Nancy said, closing the door behind her.

The mechanic raised a dark, bushy eyebrow. "What about it?" he asked, reaching over to turn down the radio.

"I think Mr. Stone's brake pipe might have been cut on purpose," Nancy said.

The man put down his coffee cup on the scarred desk. "Yeah?" he asked, frowning.

"There's a good chance," Nancy replied. "I was there when the brakes failed. My friend and I took a look under the hood, but I'd like a mechanic's opinion."

"The car's out back in the lot," the mechanic said, pointing over his shoulder with a greasy thumb. Then, picking up a flashlight, he rose from his chair. "I was going to start working on it right after my coffee break."

A short while later Nancy and the mechanic were

leaning over the engine of Nelson Stone's car. "I'd say this was cut with a hacksaw," the mechanic said, inspecting the pipe closely with a flashlight.

"How can you tell?" Nancy asked.

Suddenly the flashlight dimmed. The mechanic banged it against the engine until the beam brightened. "Look," he said, shining the beam on the metal brake pipe. "You can even see the teeth marks made by the hacksaw blade."

"Wow!" Nancy whistled softly. "You're right. I thought that was just corrosion."

"It usually is with these vintage cars," he remarked. "Let's have a look at the other brake pipe."

Just then the flashlight flickered dimly once again. The mechanic shook it and slapped it against the palm of his hand. "This thing probably needs new batteries," he said.

Nancy searched her purse. "I usually have a penlight with me," she said, "but I can't seem to find it."

"Maybe Mr. Stone has one in his glove compartment," the mechanic suggested.

Nancy moved around to the side of the car and opened the front door. But as the interior light flicked on, she jumped back with a gasp of horror.

In the dim light a woman's body was stretched facedown across the front seat, her head dangling toward the floor!

4

A Startling Surprise

Nancy stood still for a moment, wondering whether the woman was alive. She motioned for the mechanic to come over, then pointed inside the car.

At that moment the woman lifted her head. Nancy noticed that she was holding a penlight. Even in the near-dark Nancy recognized Margaret Parker's face from the graduation photo she had seen in her office earlier that day.

"Ms. Parker!" the mechanic said in surprise, looking over Nancy's shoulder. "You still here? Did you find your earring yet?"

Margaret Parker sat up in the driver's seat and pushed back her short blond hair. Then, with a curious glance at Nancy, she said, "No. Maybe I didn't lose it here, after all. I was helping my boss carry some books out of his car this morning, and . . . oh, well, never mind," she said, looking disappointed. "They were my favorite earrings."

Nancy fingered the gold earring in her jacket pocket. Could it be the same one Margaret was looking for? She couldn't be certain until she saw the mate, and she didn't see Margaret wearing it now. For a moment Nancy wrestled with her conscience, wondering if she should show it to the assistant curator. But her better judgment told her to keep quiet and hold on to the earring for the time being, in case she needed it later for evidence.

Margaret climbed out of the car. She was of medium height, with a slim figure, dressed in a neat blue suit. Turning to the mechanic, Margaret said, "Well, thanks anyway." Then she started to walk away, her high heels clicking against the asphalt like castanets.

"Just a minute, Ms. Parker!" Nancy called.

Margaret stopped and turned around. "Yes?" she asked.

"If you don't mind," Nancy said, "I'd like to ask you something."

"Who are you?" Margaret said, frowning.

Nancy stepped toward her. "I'm Nancy Drew," she explained, her hands still in her pockets. "You see, Mr. Stone is a family friend. I was with him today when the Golden Horse was stolen."

"Oh, yes," Margaret replied, her voice suddenly softer. "Wasn't that terrible? I just heard about it a little while ago."

Nancy studied Margaret's large brown eyes, trying to read beneath the surface. The young woman seemed reserved and highly intelligent. Nancy sensed that she wouldn't be rattled easily. But Margaret seemed more upset about the loss of her earring than she did over the theft of the Golden Horse. Or maybe, Nancy reasoned, the assistant curator might secretly be pleased that Nelson Stone had been placed in an embarrassing situation. After all, Hillary had mentioned that the curator didn't treat his staff very well.

"Were you at the museum earlier today?" Nancy asked pointedly.

Margaret's brown eyes gazed steadily at Nancy. "No," she answered. "I was off today."

Nancy wondered whether Margaret was lying. "So, you weren't at the museum at all today?" she pressed. "Didn't you just say that you helped your boss with some books this morning?"

Margaret bristled. "Mr. Stone dropped them by my house," she said. "Why are you giving me the third degree?"

Nancy hesitated, not wanting to reveal that she was working for Nelson Stone. The less people knew, she figured, the better her chances of getting to the truth. "I was just interested," Nancy said finally.

Margaret Parker turned on her high heels. "I see. Now, if you'll excuse me . . ."

Before Nancy could say another word, the woman hurried off.

The mechanic chuckled. "Not too friendly, huh?" he remarked, wiping his hands on an oily rag. "Maybe

39

she's just upset about losing her earring. I wouldn't take it too personally."

"I'll try not to lose any sleep over it," Nancy quipped. "Thanks for your help," she added, heading back toward her car.

Early the next morning Nancy phoned George and Bess and arranged to meet them downtown at Pancake City for breakfast.

Bess was already digging into a plate of blueberry pancakes when Nancy arrived.

"Hi, Bess," Nancy greeted her friend, sliding into the opposite seat in the booth.

Bess took a gulp of water and swallowed hard. "Hi," she said with a bright smile. "Sorry I couldn't wait to order, but I was absolutely starving." She smiled sheepishly. "You know me and my crash diets."

"Sure," Nancy said, chuckling. "You diet all week, then crash into Pancake City."

A few minutes later a redheaded waitress appeared and took Nancy's order for a toasted English muffin and a cup of black coffee.

"Is that all you're having?" Bess blurted. "No wonder you stay so thin."

"To tell you the truth," Nancy said, "I'm too excited to eat."

Bess looked at her with wide blue eyes. "Really? What happened?"

Just then Nancy saw George enter the restaurant and waved.

"Sorry, I'm late," George said breathlessly. She slipped out of her windbreaker and took the seat next to Nancy. "I couldn't get my car started, so I had to jog all the way here."

The waitress returned with Nancy's coffee and waited while George studied the menu.

"I'll have the banana pancakes and a cup of tea, please," George told her. Then, turning to Nancy, she asked, "So, what's going on?"

Nancy took a sip of coffee. "Plenty," she said. She told her friends about her visit to Rapid Repair the night before.

George frowned. "Do you think the person who cut Stone's brake pipe is the same one who sent him the threatening letter?"

"It sure seems that way," Nancy said.

Bess shook her head. "There's one thing I don't understand," she said. "The person who wrote that note—did he or she also steal the Golden Horse?"

Nancy put down her cup. "I wish I had the answer to that," she said, leaning back in her seat. "It could have been the same person. But it could also have been pure coincidence that the robbery took place right after Stone received the letter."

Nancy went on to tell Bess and George about her run-in with Margaret Parker. She opened her purse and clenched the earring in her fist. "I can't be certain until the match turns up," she said, "but I think Margaret might have been looking for this." Nancy opened her palm.

George gasped. "That's the earring you found near

the window ledge! So it must belong to Margaret Parker, right?"

"Let's say there's a good chance," Nancy said with a grin.

"That means Margaret could have stolen the Golden Horse," Bess said excitedly.

"That's right," George agreed. "Her earring probably fell off while she was escaping through the window."

"It's possible," Nancy said, buttering her English muffin. "But even if this earring *is* Margaret Parker's, she may have lost it near the window ledge last week, for all we know. Anyway, I'm going to hold on to it for now, in case it ties up with something later."

George combed her fingers through her dark curls. "It's weird that you found Margaret in the car, though. She could have been the one who cut the brake pipes, right?"

"Just because Margaret was looking for her earring in Stone's car," Nancy reminded her friend, "doesn't necessarily connect her with any foul play."

"Besides," Bess added, "why would Stone's assistant want to kill him?"

Nancy cupped her face in her hands. "Right now, I'm not sure. But there's someone else at the top of my list who might have a reason. It's possible Hillary Lane wrote the threatening letter to Mr. Stone *and* stole the Golden Horse."

Nancy told her friends what she'd learned from her father and Hannah about the former actress.

"It's hard to imagine Hillary Lane as a museum curator," George remarked.

"She looks too glamorous," Bess said.

Nancy smiled. "Maybe there's a side to Hillary that we don't know."

A short while later, after leaving Bess to do some shopping, Nancy offered George a lift to the River Heights Country Club.

As they drove, George said, "So, if Hillary was qualified to be curator, but Nelson Stone got the job instead, it's possible that she wrote the letter to scare Stone out of town. Maybe she stole the Golden Horse to finish the job of ruining his reputation."

"I had the same thought," Nancy said, nodding. "Hillary Lane had enough time to slip out of the reference library, pass Stone's closed office door, and make her way into the Tibetan section. She could have stolen the artifact and returned to the library before Stone came out of his office. Of course, there's a chance she could have been hiding in the assistant curator's office. And if that red purse is hers—"

"There's only one problem," George broke in. "How could Hillary have known that the case was going to be open?"

"It was highly unlikely," Nancy agreed. "But maybe she had a duplicate key to the case, and the fact that Stone had left it open was just pure coincidence."

A few minutes later Nancy dropped George off at the country club. "Don't forget," George reminded Nancy, "Bess and I want tickets for the dog show, too. We'll pay you back later, okay?"

43

"No problem," Nancy said. Then, making a U-turn, she stuck her head out the window and called, "I'll pick you up here around one o'clock."

Soon Nancy had arrived at Hillary Lane's palatial estate and parked her car in the circular driveway. She walked up the wide, stone steps to the stately white house. It was a tall, white-pillared building, surrounded by blossoming trees and a wide expanse of lawn.

Nancy rang the bell. A moment later the butler opened the heavy oak door. After Nancy introduced herself, the butler reached into his breast pocket and produced an envelope. "Miss Lane said to tell you that the ticket is complimentary."

"Thank you very much," Nancy said.

The butler was about to close the door.

"Wait," Nancy said. "I—"

"Yes?" the butler said. "Was there something else?"

"I'd love to thank Ms. Lane myself," Nancy told him.

The butler nodded. "I'll be sure to do that for you," he replied politely.

Nancy pressed her hand against the door. "I mean, I really would like to thank her *personally*," she said.

The butler pursed his lips. "Ms. Lane is not available at the moment," he said firmly.

Nancy thought quickly. "But I'd like to buy some extra tickets for my friends," she said.

The butler sighed. "Oh, very well," he said impatiently, ushering Nancy into the foyer. He led her toward the morning room. "If you'll just wait here, I'll get the tickets for you."

Nancy paced the polished floor and gazed out the tall French windows. On the lawn beside a duck pond a number of workmen were raising a green and white striped tent. The tent was probably for the dog show, Nancy told herself.

Suddenly two white poodles came running into the room. Nancy bent down to pat their curly white heads as they sniffed her feet.

"Marcus! Chloe!" she heard a woman call. The poodles sat at attention as Hillary Lane entered the room. She was dressed casually in jeans and a red sweater. Her blond hair was pulled back in a French braid, and she wore hardly any makeup. Nancy thought the heiress could almost pass for a teenager.

"Nancy Drew!" Hillary said. "What a nice surprise."

"Good morning," Nancy said. "Thanks for the ticket."

"Oh, no problem," Hillary replied, lifting a poodle into her arms. "Your father has been such a help to me. And I know you'll really love the dog show." She put down the poodle, and it scampered off with its mate.

"Actually, I'd like to buy two extra tickets for my friends," Nancy explained. "I'll pay for them, of course," she added quickly.

"Come along into the study," Hillary said, "and I'll get them for you."

Nancy followed Hillary through the impressive

entrance hall. The walls were lined with large oil paintings of men and women from another era, who seemed to stare down at Nancy from ornate gilded frames as she passed. Probably Hillary's ancestors, Nancy thought.

To her left, Nancy saw a dining room furnished with a long mahogany table and a hutch that housed gold-rimmed plates. The table's surface reflected, mirrorlike, the crystal chandelier overhead.

"You have a beautiful home," Nancy said as they passed the living room, filled with Oriental rugs, thick drapes, velvet sofas, and a grand piano.

"Thank you," the heiress said with a sigh. "But to tell you the truth, the only house I ever really loved was the Lane mansion. All the Lanes were born there. It really should have been kept in the family." Her expression darkened. "I get so angry every time I think of Nelson Stone and all those ugly renovations he's planning to make to my family home. And he has absolutely no regard for my opinion," Hillary went on. "You heard the way he spoke to me when I was in his office. What were you doing there, by the way?"

"Oh, Mr. Stone invited me to see the Tibetan exhibit," she fibbed. "He's a family friend."

Hillary twisted her gold link necklace with an index finger. "They'll never find the Golden Horse," she said. "Can you imagine? How irresponsible of Nelson Stone, leaving the case unlocked."

They entered a dark, oak-paneled study lined with

books on Oriental art. The heiress offered Nancy a seat.

Suddenly Nancy noticed a box of Gold Flag chocolates lying on the side table. Her mind flashed back to the box of Gold Flag chocolates Nelson Stone had received. Could there be a connection? It was hard to imagine Hillary sending Stone a present.

Nancy glanced up at the leather-bound books. "You must know a lot about Oriental art," Nancy said, hoping to draw Hillary out.

"I have a passion for Oriental art," Hillary said. "It's my greatest love."

"I'm becoming very interested in the subject myself," Nancy told her.

Hillary Lane pulled a large volume off the shelf and handed it to Nancy. "This book is on antique Japanese dolls. I edited the manuscript," she added.

Nancy opened the book. "What magnificent dolls," she remarked, looking at the full-page photographs.

The heiress leaned over Nancy's shoulder. "Some of those dolls are part of my private collection."

"Oh, I'd love to see them," Nancy said. "Is there any chance I could?"

Hillary hesitated. "Well, actually—I'm in the process of reorganizing . . ." she hedged.

"Could I see just a few of the dolls?" Nancy asked sweetly.

Hillary hesitated once again, twisting her gold-crest pinkie ring. "Well, perhaps just the dolls," she agreed finally.

Nancy followed Hillary down a carpeted hallway, its walls covered with beige silk. They soon reached a large, heavy, oak-carved door with a polished brass doorknob and several locks.

"I don't take many people here," Hillary said. "It's sort of my secret place, where I like to meditate. It's very serene and . . . well, you'll see in a minute." Pushing open the door, she flicked on the floodlights.

"Wow!" Nancy said as she entered. The room was enormous, containing many glass cases filled with Oriental treasures. The far wall was lined with tapestries. To her left, Nancy saw several colorful paintings, similar to the Indian miniatures she'd noticed on the second floor of the Clinton Park Museum.

Hillary waved a hand toward a group of glass cases on the right wall. "Those are my precious Japanese dolls."

Nancy looked over the white-faced, traditionally dressed figures, seated serenely inside the cases. "They're really lovely," she remarked.

"I'm afraid I haven't shown my treasures to anyone for a while," Hillary confessed. The heiress closed her eyes for a brief moment, and Nancy sensed she was off in her own private world. Turning toward the tapestries, Nancy noticed a glass case containing small Buddhist statues.

"Oh, those are just my Chinese tapestries," Hillary said with a shrug.

"Actually, the Buddhas caught my eye," Nancy told her. "Do you mind if I take a look at them?"

Before Hillary had time to reply, Nancy stepped toward the statues. But as she reached the case, she froze. On a shelf, right behind the Buddhas, stood the dazzling Golden Horse!

5

Conflicting Clues

"It's the Golden Horse!" Nancy cried in disbelief.

Hillary Lane's eyes sparkled. "Yes," she said with a sigh. "Isn't it lovely?"

Nancy stared at the heiress, wondering if the woman was insane. How else, Nancy reasoned, could the heiress steal a priceless treasure, then behave as if nothing were wrong?

Nancy dug her nails into the palms of her hands. How do I handle this one? she thought as Hillary came over and stood beside her. "Such a pity!" Hillary said. "I would have loved to have had the pair."

Nancy frowned. "What do you mean?" she asked.

"There are two Golden Horses, you know," Hillary went on breezily. "They were originally a set."

Nancy breathed a silent sigh of relief.

"You see," Hillary went on, "the Golden Horses were split up and smuggled out of Tibet when the Chinese invaded the country in 1950." Hillary stepped forward and stroked the statue, as if it were a pet. "I bought this one in Hong Kong a few years ago. I would love to have the second one. But when the other came up for auction last month, Nelson Stone outbid me. I just couldn't get my hands on a million in cash," she added with a shrug.

"How interesting," Nancy said, thinking how angry Hillary must have been to lose the other Golden Horse to Stone.

Several minutes later Hillary completed the tour of her private museum. "I'd love to ask you to stay for lunch, Nancy," she said, relocking the oak doors, "but the cook is off today."

"Thank you," Nancy said as they moved down the carpeted hallway. "I really should be on my way."

"We'll do it another time," Hillary said. They neared the study, and the heiress suddenly snapped her fingers. "Oh, I nearly forgot all about your tickets."

Nancy followed Hillary into the study and took a seat in a brown leather chair as Hillary rummaged through a small antique desk. "Ah, here they are," she said, handing Nancy two yellow tickets. Nancy gave her two twenty-dollar bills, and Hillary excused herself to get change. But before leaving the room, she picked up the box of Gold Flag chocolates and offered them to Nancy. "Have a treat while you wait," she said with a smile. "I'll be right back."

"Oh, thanks," Nancy said, taking the box from Hillary. As the heiress left the room, Nancy picked out a caramel. Hillary Lane was definitely more generous with her chocolates than Nelson Stone was.

A few minutes later the heiress returned to the study with a red lizard purse. "Here's your change, Nancy," she said, handing over a ten-dollar bill.

Nancy stared at the red purse.

"Is something wrong?" Hillary asked, arching her eyebrows.

Nancy blinked. "Oh, no," she said. "Nothing at all."

Nancy was still thinking about the red purse as she left Hillary Lane's house. Was it the same purse she'd seen in Margaret Parker's office just before the robbery? It was the first thing she told George about when they met for lunch at the country club.

"Boy!" George said, shaking her head. Her hair was still damp from a shower. "Hillary's looking more suspicious by the minute." George bit into her grilled cheese sandwich and chewed thoughtfully for a moment. "Do you think she's telling the truth about there being two Golden Horses?"

"We can easily check on that," Nancy said. She took a bite of a french fry and told George more about her visit with the heiress. Then, pouring ketchup on

52

her hamburger, Nancy asked, "So, how did the tennis game go this morning?"

"Not too well," George confessed, making a face. "I lost in straight sets. I guess I didn't get enough sleep last night."

"Up late watching that tennis tournament on TV?" Nancy teased.

George shook her head. "No, the tournament's on tonight at eight." She grinned. "I bet Bess is miffed that 'Wheel of Chance,' that game show she watches every week, will be preempted. Actually, I was lying awake thinking about the robbery. I've been racking my brain, trying to remember that car I saw leaving the museum."

"Don't worry," Nancy told her friend. "When you stop trying, you'll remember."

"I hope so," George said.

After lunch Nancy stopped at a pay phone and punched in Nelson Stone's number.

"Nelson Stone's office," a woman answered.

Nancy recognized Margaret Parker's throaty voice. "May I speak with him, please?" she asked. "This is Nancy Drew calling."

"Mr. Stone is at lunch," Margaret replied crisply. "Would you care to leave a message?"

Nancy made a quick decision not to ask Margaret any questions about the Golden Horse. "No, thanks," she replied. "Is Su-Lin there, by any chance?"

"Ms. Tung is only in on weekends," the assistant curator said.

"Okay," Nancy said. "I'll call back later."

After getting Su-Lin's home phone number from directory assistance, Nancy punched in the second call. The phone rang for a long time. Just as Nancy was about to hang up, Su-Lin answered. Her voice sounded teary, as if she'd been crying.

"Su-Lin, it's Nancy Drew. Are you all right?"

"Not really," Su-Lin said, sniffling. "I just came home from school and learned that my father lost his job."

"That's awful," Nancy said. "He's such a wonderful gardener."

Su-Lin sighed. "Working on the Lane estate was my father's whole life. He's never even worked anywhere else in this country."

"But why was he fired?" Nancy asked.

Su-Lin cleared her throat. "I think Mr. Stone got upset because something was missing in the toolshed," she said. "It sounds so ridiculous. But I guess Mr. Stone lost his temper."

Nancy wondered why a curator would be so concerned about a missing gardening tool.

"Do you think your father would mind if I came over and talked to him?" Nancy asked. Any unusual happening at the museum seemed worth investigating. And maybe there was something she could do to help.

"Oh, Nancy. That's so nice of you," Su-Lin replied. "I don't know how to comfort my father. It might cheer him up a bit to have a guest." She gave Nancy her address, and Nancy promised to come right over.

Nancy dropped George off at her house. Then she continued on to the Tungs' place, a small garden apartment in the downtown section of Clinton Park. Su-Lin waved through an open window as Nancy drove up.

"Hi," Nancy called, getting out of the car.

"Come on in," Su-Lin said. "My father's in the living room. I'll make us all a pot of tea."

"Sounds great," Nancy said, following Su-Lin into the neatly furnished apartment. Lee Tung was sitting in a wicker armchair, gazing out the window.

"Ms. Drew," the gardener said, rising.

"I hope I'm not disturbing you, Mr. Tung," Nancy said as Su-Lin disappeared into the kitchen.

"No, no," Lee Tung replied, motioning for Nancy to have a seat on the couch. Then, dropping back into his chair, he sighed. "Now I have all the time in the world, I'm afraid."

"I'm sorry to hear you lost your job," Nancy said.

For a moment there was a silence, broken only by the rattle of teacups in the kitchen.

"Yes," the old gardener said finally. "But, to tell you the truth, I haven't really been happy there since Mr. Stone was hired."

"What do you think his problem is?" Nancy asked.

"He has a short temper," the gardener replied. "And he always thinks he's right."

"Can you give me an example?" Nancy asked. She had to be sure whether Lee Tung's grievances were real or imaginary.

"Well, take this incident of his firing me," Lee Tung

said, pulling his chair closer to Nancy. "The man had no business nosing around my things. But he was all upset when he learned that one of my tools was found near the parking lot. I had put the tool away, but then Mr. Stone came around and wanted to know where it was. For some reason, I just couldn't find it. That's when he got angry."

"What kind of a tool was it?" Nancy asked.

"Just an old hacksaw," Lee Tung replied with a shrug.

A sudden chill ran up Nancy's spine. "A hacksaw?" she echoed.

At that moment Su-Lin appeared from the kitchen, carrying a china tea set on a black lacquered tray. "The whole thing was so unfair," Su-Lin said. She put the tray down on a low table and began to pour the jasmine-scented tea.

Nancy took the teacup from Su-Lin and turned to Lee Tung. She definitely needed to get a look at the hacksaw. Maybe it was the same one that had been used to cut Stone's brake pipe, she thought. But why had the curator been looking for it? Maybe the mechanic had told Nelson Stone how the brake pipe had been cut.

Nancy leaned forward. "Mr. Tung," she said, "do you think I might be able to find the hacksaw in the shed?" She wanted to see if there was any trace of oil on the blade of the hacksaw—it just might match the brake fluid in Stone's car. But she also had another reason to find the lost tool. "Maybe if I find the hacksaw," she added, "I can persuade Mr. Stone to give you back your job. I guess he's been under a lot of strain lately."

"That's true," Su-Lin said, nodding.

Lee Tung smiled hopefully at his daughter. "Maybe Nancy *can* help us," he said. "I'll get my jacket and come along."

"You'd better stay home," Su-Lin warned her father. "Remember, Mr. Stone ordered you never to step foot on the premises again."

"Don't worry," Nancy said. "I'll be fine alone."

Lee Tung gave Nancy a spare key to the toolshed. "Be sure to give us a call when you get back," he said.

"Don't worry about the time," Su-Lin added as she and her father walked Nancy to the door. "We'll be waiting to hear from you."

Shortly after dark Nancy arrived at the Clinton Park Museum. Passing the main gate, she saw that it was locked. She then quickly turned off into a dark lane and parked her car.

Nancy took a pair of wire cutters from the trunk, then moved quietly between the trees. The moon provided just enough light to see the way.

Soon Nancy came to a tall wire-mesh fence that surrounded the museum. She bent down and started to snip a hole in the fence with the wire cutters.

It wasn't long before Nancy had cut a hole large enough to crawl through. Then she darted across the lawn, hoping she wouldn't be spotted by a night watchman.

Reaching the back of the museum, Nancy stood in a shadow and caught her breath. Had she heard footsteps on the gravel driveway behind her? She listened intently, but the only sound was an owl hooting in the night.

Cautiously Nancy inched her way along the side of the museum. She could see the toolshed just a few yards away, bathed in moonlight. Nancy hesitated to cross the open ground.

A moment later a cloud passed in front of the moon. Nancy dashed across to the shed and pressed against the door. For a second she fumbled in her pocket for the key. Then, slipping it into the lock, she turned it slowly.

The lock clicked open, and Nancy pushed the door back. She slipped inside and illuminated the shed with her penlight.

Nancy saw a long workbench on one side of the room. Above it was a rack of garden tools. Glancing underneath the bench, she spied a toolbox. "That's as good a place as any to start looking," she muttered to herself.

Sliding the metal toolbox toward her, Nancy lifted the lid. At first all she could see was a rack of small tools and nuts and bolts. No hacksaw here, she thought.

Nancy flashed her light beneath the bench, but the only other thing she could find was a wicker basket filled with hedge clippers and a worn pair of gardening gloves.

This is turning out to be fruitless, Nancy decided. Frustrated, she pulled at the top tray of the toolbox. To her surprise it lifted up, and a hacksaw was lying under the hammer! Quickly Nancy took a clean white handkerchief from her pocket and wrapped it carefully around the handle of the hacksaw. Then, lifting the saw from the toolbox, she ran her penlight along the serrated edge.

"I knew it," Nancy told herself. "Just what I was looking for." She could see a slight sheen of brake fluid still clinging to the blade.

Taking a magnifying glass from her pocket, Nancy inspected the blade closely. Tiny dots of metal filings shone in the light. I'll bet these filings match the metal of Stone's brake pipe, she thought.

Nancy replaced the toolbox, her heart pounding as she left the shed with the hacksaw. She had to get the hacksaw to a forensic laboratory and have the metal filings and brake fluid analyzed. The wooden handle of the saw could also be checked for fingerprints. Both Nelson Stone and Lee Tung had handled the hacksaw, of course. But maybe another suspect would enter the spotlight.

Nancy turned to relock the door. Suddenly someone grabbed the hacksaw from her hand and pushed her violently inside the shed!

6

The Necklace

"Hey!" Nancy cried as she fell to the floor of the toolshed. The door slammed shut behind her, and she heard the sharp click of the lock.

Nancy got up and rushed to the door. She tried to pull it open, but she quickly realized it was hopeless. Her mind raced as she tried to imagine who had locked her inside the shed. Nancy was almost certain she had felt a man's large hand against her back. If only she had turned in time to see his face, she thought. Whoever it was must have been desperate to get hold of the hacksaw.

Nancy flashed her penlight around the shed again, looking for another way out. In the back, above the workbench, she saw a small window.

Nancy climbed onto the bench and struggled to lift the window. The opening seemed just large enough for her to squeeze through. Leaning out, she estimated it was a six-foot drop to the ground.

Nancy reached up and gripped the metal gutter under the edge of the roof. She swung her legs out and took a deep breath, ready to jump. Suddenly the gutter ripped away from its fastening. Nancy grabbed desperately at the roof, but her hand slipped and she fell awkwardly onto the hard ground.

Nancy got up slowly and felt a sharp pain in her left ankle. Probably a sprain, she thought as she moved forward. She limped across the front lawn, toward her car. Her assailant was probably long gone.

Finally Nancy reached her Mustang. She was just about to get in when she heard the rush of footsteps behind her.

Nancy swung around, crouching low in a karate stance, prepared to defend herself. The sudden movement sent a sharp pain shooting up her left leg, and she winced.

A moment later she was relieved to see Lee Tung heading toward her in the moonlight.

"Oh, there you are, Nancy," the gardener said. "As soon as you left, I realized I shouldn't have let you come here alone."

Nancy grimaced and bent down to rub her ankle. "I'm afraid I haven't had much luck."

"You couldn't find the hacksaw?" he asked.

"I found it, all right," Nancy replied grimly. She told Lee Tung what had happened.

61

The gardener listened in horror. "Let me take you to a hospital," he said finally. "A doctor should check that ankle."

"Thanks, but I'll be fine," Nancy told him. "All I need is a cold compress to relieve the swelling."

"Then leave your car here until morning," Lee Tung said. "I'll drive you home." He guided Nancy slowly down the road to his pickup truck. "We can stop at my house on the way. Su-Lin will give you a strong cup of ginseng tea and an herbal balm to relieve the pain in your ankle."

As they drove away from the museum, Lee Tung said, "My job was so much better when I worked for Amanda Lane. I designed all the formal gardens. There were always lawn parties and happy times, especially when Hillary Lane was around. She was like a royal princess, and the Lane mansion was her castle."

Nancy imagined Hillary as a young debutante, the star of every social event. "I guess the Lane estate must hold many wonderful memories for Hillary," Nancy remarked.

"Yes," Lee Tung said. "I think that must be why she comes to the museum so often. Sometimes she sits outside, staring at the mansion."

When they arrived at the garden apartment, a concerned Su-Lin helped Nancy into the living room and settled her on the couch. In a few minutes Nancy was sipping a strong cup of ginseng tea.

Su-Lin applied a compress of herbal balm to Nancy's ankle. "This should help," she told her.

Lee Tung came into the room to check on Nancy, then returned to his bedroom to watch the end of the tennis tournament on TV.

"I feel terrible," Su-Lin said. "If it weren't for my father's problem, you would never have gone out to the museum and been attacked."

"It's not your fault," Nancy assured her. "Besides, I'm used to these things. Sometimes I do detective work," she added.

Su-Lin's face brightened. "Oh, Nancy. I didn't know you were a detective. Maybe you can help find the Golden Horse."

Nancy took another sip of tea. "I'm sure the police are working on it," she said. "But I've been making some inquiries on my own. By the way," she added casually, "are there *two* Golden Horses?"

Su-Lin's face brightened with interest. "Oh, yes, of course," she said. "Originally, they were a pair. If you want to know more about them, my anthropology professor has written a good book on Tibetan artifacts. It has a whole chapter devoted to the history of the Golden Horses. I'm sure Professor Herbert wouldn't mind showing it to you."

"That sounds like a great idea."

Nancy said good night to Lee Tung and thanked him for his help before following Su-Lin out front to her car. As Su-Lin drove Nancy home, she talked more about her anthropology courses at Westmoor University. "Professor Herbert is an expert in the field," she said. "I feel very lucky to be studying with him."

"Could you do me a favor?" Nancy asked as they pulled up to her house.

"Sure," Su-Lin replied.

"See if you can find out if Margaret Parker has a red purse," Nancy said.

Su-Lin sighed. "I don't know whether I'll be working at the museum anymore, since Mr. Stone fired my father."

Nancy shook her head. "Please try to stay on a little while longer," she said. "You might be able to find an important clue for me. Just think of yourself as an undercover agent." Su-Lin hesitated.

"I really need your help," Nancy urged. "Maybe if we work together, we can help find the Golden Horse."

Finally Su-Lin nodded. "Okay," she said. Then she raised her hands to the back of her neck and withdrew a beautiful jade and silver necklace from under her blouse. "I'd like you to wear this while you're on the case," she said, handing the necklace to Nancy. "It was given to my great-grandmother by her husband as a wedding gift. It is traditional for Tibetan brides to be given necklaces like this. There have been lovely stories passed down in our family about this necklace. They say no one can harm the person who wears it."

"It's absolutely magnificent," Nancy said as she held the necklace up. A large silver locket hung from a strand of jade and silver beads. Fascinated, Nancy took the oval object into her hand and admired its ornate engraving. "But I couldn't possibly borrow such a precious heirloom," she said, frowning.

"Please," Su-Lin insisted. "It will protect you. Besides, it will make me happy if you wear it."

"All right," Nancy said. "Thank you very much. I'll be very careful with it."

As Nancy slipped the necklace over her head, Su-Lin said, "There is one thing I must warn you of. You must never open the locket."

Nancy nodded. "All right," she agreed. "Do you mind my asking why?"

Su-Lin grinned. "Just trust me," she said. "It's a family secret."

As Nancy got out of the car, she turned and gave Su-Lin a pat on the shoulder. "Thanks again for everything," she said.

At seven o'clock the next morning Nancy took a cab out to the museum and picked up her car. Shortly after she returned home, the phone rang.

"Yes, Mr. Stone," she said, recognizing the curator's nervous voice. "I'm glad you called. There were a few things I wanted to ask you about."

"Well, I'm rather shook up at the moment," he said. "My neighbor's spaniel is very ill."

"I'm sorry to hear that," Nancy said. "Is the dog going to be all right?"

"I don't care about the animal," he snapped. "It's *me* I'm worried about."

"Are you sick, too?" Nancy asked politely.

"No, no. I didn't eat the Gold Flag chocolates. Rusty did," Mr. Stone said.

"You mean you gave a dog chocolates?" Nancy said in disbelief. She remembered how the curator hadn't offered any of his candies to Bess.

"*I* didn't give them to him," Mr. Stone explained impatiently. "Rusty stole the chocolates out of the garbage can. You see, I just didn't feel safe eating them. I didn't even know who they were from. For all I knew, the chocolates could have been poisoned. So I threw the box out. Rusty must have found it in the garbage can."

"How can I help you?" Nancy asked.

"The point is," Mr. Stone said, "that I'm sure those chocolates were poisoned. I tell you, someone's trying to kill me."

"Please calm down, Mr. Stone," Nancy replied. "Any dog that eats a whole box of chocolates is going to be sick. It doesn't necessarily mean the chocolates were poisoned."

"Dr. Morgan at the animal clinic pumped Rusty's stomach in case of food poisoning last night," Mr. Stone insisted.

Nancy bit her lip. Maybe the chocolates were poisoned after all. "I'll look into it," she said, making a mental note to phone Dr. Morgan herself. "By the way," she added, "I was just wondering. . . . Where were you last night?"

"Why, here at home," Mr. Stone answered. "I always watch 'Wheel of Chance' on Thursday nights. Wouldn't miss it."

Nancy had a hard time picturing the stuffy curator watching a TV game show. She said goodbye to Mr. Stone, agreeing to keep in touch. She wanted to talk to him about the hacksaw, of course, but she'd decided to wait until later, when she could see his reaction in person. There was something about Nelson Stone's manner that didn't seem quite right.

It was still too early to phone the vet, so Nancy went upstairs, sat down at her desk, and scribbled some notes in her spiral notebook.

Nancy turned to a clean page and printed "STONE." Underneath she wrote:

1. Receives threatening letter
2. Brake pipe cut with hacksaw—brakes fail
3. Looks for hacksaw in toolshed—gardener fired
4. N.D. locked inside toolshed—hacksaw stolen
5. Dog poisoned after eating chocolates sent to Stone
6. Curator watches "Wheel of Chance" regularly?

Suddenly Nancy sat up straighter. Remembering her conversation with George at the club, she ran downstairs and grabbed a newspaper. She thumbed through the TV listings, until she found what she was looking for. "Aha!" she cried. " 'Wheel of Chance' was canceled last night for the tennis tournament. Nelson Stone was lying!"

7

A Setup

Nancy threw down the newspaper. "I can't believe it!" she exclaimed. She wondered if Nelson Stone had been at the museum the night before. Could the curator have been the one who had locked her in the toolshed?

A short while later Nancy was on the phone with Rusty's vet. But after a brief conversation with Dr. Morgan, all she had learned was that the spaniel had been poisoned and would recover. But since Rusty had finished the box of Gold Flag, there was no way to prove the poison was in the chocolates. "It could have been in any of the garbage he ate," the vet pointed out.

Nancy hung up and thought for a moment. She'd

have to find out who had actually sent Nelson Stone the package. What she needed now was an expert in chocolates.

Quickly she called Bess, who told Nancy that there were only two shops in the local area that carried the exclusive Gold Flag brand.

An hour later Nancy met Bess at the mall, and the two of them headed toward the Candy Boutique.

"You have to understand," Bess told Nancy as they neared the gourmet candy shop, "that this is a dangerous place for me when I'm on a diet."

Nancy quickened her pace. "Come on, Bess. We're not going there to buy candy," she reminded her friend. "We have to find out who sent Mr. Stone those chocolates."

The girls entered the trendy shop, which was decorated in chrome and glass. Nancy walked up to the counter, while Bess browsed around. "May I speak with the manager?" Nancy asked the young saleswoman.

"The manager is off today," the woman replied. "Is there something I can help you with?"

Nancy decided to keep her story simple. "My friend received a box of Gold Flag chocolates in the mail the other day," she began. "But the card was missing and he's terribly embarrassed. He doesn't know whom to thank."

The woman shrugged. "We don't keep records on customers," she said. "There's no way to check something like that."

Nancy glanced over at Bess, who was eyeing the

candy on display. But just as she was about to leave, an idea flashed into her mind. "Would you happen to know Hillary Lane?" Nancy asked.

"Of course," the saleswoman replied. "Everyone in town knows Hillary Lane. She's a regular customer here."

"Would you know if she sent a box of Gold Flag chocolates to a Mr. Nelson Stone recently?"

"Well," the woman said, "Gold Flag *is* a favorite of Miss Lane's. But I haven't a clue as to whom she gives them. We don't mail packages for our customers."

"Thanks anyway for your help," Nancy said as she and Bess left the shop. If Hillary had bought the chocolates and then sent them to Stone herself, it could be pretty difficult to prove.

Soon Nancy and Bess were heading toward Miss Rubie's Chocolate Shoppe in downtown Clinton Park.

"You realize," Bess said as they neared the shop, "that I'm doomed as soon as I walk into Miss Rubie's. I can't resist her homemade fudge."

"We'll get you some," Nancy promised.

When they entered the old-fashioned candy shop, which was decorated to look like the inside of a log cabin, Miss Rubie gave Bess a warm welcome. "Why, Bess Marvin! You must have smelled my homemade fudge all the way from River Heights," the plump proprietress said. "I just made a fresh batch this morning."

Nancy laughed. "Bess has a sixth sense for things like that."

70

Bess flashed Nancy a sheepish grin, then purchased a small box of fudge. "I'm only doing this to help you," she whispered to Nancy. Then, turning to Miss Rubie, Bess asked, "Do you still mail out gifts for your customers?"

"Of course," Miss Rubie replied. "I mail gifts all over the country."

"Actually," Bess said, "we were wondering about something. By any chance, did you send a package recently to a Mr. Nelson Stone here in Clinton Park?"

"I'll have to check my records," Miss Rubie said, putting on her glasses. "My memory's not as good as it used to be." She reached into a drawer behind the counter and pulled out a small box filled with postal receipts.

Nancy flashed Bess a hopeful look as Miss Rubie thumbed through the stack of papers. "This is it," she said finally. "A box of Gold Flag was sent to Mr. Stone last Friday." Miss Rubie passed the postal slip over to Nancy. "Here, take a look."

Now we're getting somewhere, Nancy thought. All she needed now was to find out who had made the purchase.

"But this doesn't say who sent it," Nancy said, disappointed. She handed the postal slip to Bess.

"It's important that we find out who sent the package," Bess explained to Miss Rubie.

"Oh, I wouldn't know that," the plump woman said. "I don't even put customers' names on sales slips."

Nancy wasn't about to give up. "What about credit card receipts?" she asked. "Names always appear on them."

Miss Rubie searched through another box. "Well, these are the only credit card charges I had last week." She handed Nancy a small pile of yellow slips.

The girls looked through them quickly.

"Hey, check this out," Bess said suddenly. "Nelson Stone charged a box of Gold Flag last Thursday."

"That's weird," Nancy said, frowning. "Could Stone have sent *himself* the box of chocolates?"

"Oh, now I remember," Miss Rubie said, leaning over the counter. "A short man, well dressed . . . very precise, as I recall."

Bess flashed Nancy a knowing look.

"That's him," Nancy said.

After thanking Miss Rubie for her help, the girls left the candy shop and got into Nancy's car.

"I just don't understand it," Bess said as Nancy pulled out of the parking lot. "Why would Nelson Stone send the chocolates to his house? He must have poisoned them himself."

Nancy turned onto the main highway. "It looks as if he rigged the whole thing," she said grimly. "He's been setting it up to look as if someone's out to kill him. What I want to know is, why?"

Bess undid the ribbon on her box of fudge. "So then Stone must have sent himself the threatening letter, too."

"And cut his own brake pipe," Nancy added as Bess offered her some fudge. "That means he probably used the hacksaw after all." She bit into a piece of fudge and chewed it thoughtfully.

"Nancy!" Bess cried. "Stone must be the one who locked you in the shed. That's terrible!"

"It sure is," Nancy agreed. "But we can't prove anything yet. I want to take another look at that threatening letter he supposedly received. Feel like driving over to the Clinton Park police station?" she asked.

"Sure," Bess said, taking another piece of fudge.

A few minutes later Nancy left Bess on the steps of the police station. "I hope you don't mind waiting," she told her friend. "It might be better if I spoke to Lieutenant Higgins alone."

"No problem," Bess said.

Nancy entered the building, hoping the lieutenant was in. "May I speak to Lieutenant Higgins, please?" she asked the bald-headed sergeant at the front desk.

"What's your name, miss?" he asked.

"Nancy Drew," she replied.

"And what is this in connection with?" he asked.

"I may have some information for the lieutenant," Nancy explained. "It's about the robbery at the museum."

The sergeant raised an eyebrow. "Just a moment, Miss Drew." He picked up the phone on his desk, punched a button on the console, and gave her message to Lieutenant Higgins. A few moments later he replaced the receiver. "Down the corridor, Miss Drew," he said finally. "It's the third door on the left."

73

Nancy knocked on the lieutenant's open door, and he motioned her inside the office. "Have a seat, Miss Drew," he said. Then he leaned across the desk. "I happened to speak with Chief McGinnis over in River Heights last night. He spoke very highly of you."

Nancy held back a smile. "We've worked together a few times," she said.

"So he told me," Higgins replied. "In fact, he seems to think that if anyone can solve this case, it's you."

"So, how are things going with the case?" Nancy asked, glancing around the sparsely furnished room. The pale green walls were filled with posters of suspects and missing persons and several framed newspaper clippings.

"Not too well," Lieutenant Higgins admitted, looking at his cluttered desk. He clasped his hands together. "So what is this information you have for me?"

"It's about the threatening letter Nelson Stone received," Nancy told him. "I'd like to take another look at it, if you don't mind."

"I thought you came here to give *me* information," Lieutenant Higgins told her. "We've already determined that there's no link between the letter and the robbery."

"I don't think we should close the door on that possibility," Nancy told him. "But, anyway, Mr. Stone wanted me to find out who had sent him the threatening letter." She had already made up her mind not to reveal her theory that Stone had been staging the attempts on his own life. "If the letter isn't part of your investigation," Nancy added, "would you mind if I had a copy of it?"

A sour expression spread across the lieutenant's face. But he took the letter from the file cabinet and made her a photocopy.

As Nancy thanked him and started out the door, Lieutenant Higgins called, "Remember to let me know if you come across any information on the robbery."

"Sure thing," Nancy promised, tucking the letter into her bag.

Rejoining Bess on the steps of the police station, Nancy said, "I've got it."

Inside the car Nancy unfolded the typed letter and read it out loud. "'To Nelson Stone,'" it began. "'This letter is not a joke, but it is written by someone who will take pleasure in destroying you. The way you run the museum and treat your staff is disgusting,'" Nancy continued reading. "'You are a bully and a snob. We don't need you in Clinton Park. Get out of town if you value your life.'" Nancy put the letter down on her lap, wondering what had been going on in Nelson Stone's mind when he composed the letter.

"So, what do you think?" Bess asked.

"Well, there's a lot of evidence that indicates that Stone wrote this letter himself," Nancy said slowly. "For some reason, he wants us to think that someone's out to kill him."

Nancy sighed. Why had Nelson Stone dragged her

into this dead-end case? She studied the type of the letter carefully.

"Look at this," she said, frowning. "All the *t*'s are marked by a distinctive break. If I could get my hands on this typewriter, I could prove that Stone wrote this letter to himself. I'm going to outsmart Nelson Stone at his own game!"

8

A Gala Event

"It's time Nelson Stone and I had a talk," Nancy said grimly.

"Are we heading out to the museum?" Bess asked as they left the police station parking lot.

"No," Nancy said. "I think I'd rather catch Stone off-guard at the dog show tomorrow."

"He's sure to be there," Bess said, nodding. "It's one of the biggest social events of the year."

The next day the girls drove out to Hillary Lane's estate. Nancy and Bess filled George in on the case's new developments.

"I can't believe it," George said. "Stone sure has

77

gone to a lot of trouble to keep you busy, Nancy. What is he up to?"

"I'm not quite sure," Nancy admitted. "But he's been making me look like a fool, and I'm determined to find out the truth about him."

When Nancy turned into Hillary Lane's driveway a few minutes later, a man wearing a red blazer collected their tickets and directed them to the crowded parking area ahead.

"They're certainly getting a good turnout," George remarked.

In the distance Nancy saw the large green and white striped refreshment tent. Beside it, a wide expanse of lawn was roped off for the arena. And all around there were well-dressed people milling about, some with dogs on leashes.

"It looks as though everyone in town is here," Bess remarked as they searched for a parking space.

"Everyone and his dog," George quipped.

At the far end of the gravel parking area, Nancy finally found an empty space. "I just hope Nelson Stone is here," she said.

George frowned as she got out of the car. "I hope I'm wearing the right thing."

Bess giggled. "For a rodeo, maybe."

"I happen to like my denim miniskirt," her cousin said defensively.

Bess tossed back her long blond hair and adjusted her wide-brimmed hat. "I hope I don't look too dressy in this flower-print dress."

78

Nancy smiled. "You look—"

"Just like Little Bo Peep," George finished.

Nancy laughed. She herself had chosen a jade-green knit dress, which matched Su-Lin's necklace perfectly.

"Look at that woman over there in the huge white hat," Bess said. "You see, I'm not *that* overdressed."

"That's Margaret Parker," Nancy said.

"Where?" George asked, craning her neck as they neared the arena.

"The young woman in the red dress," Nancy said in a low voice. "You can't miss her."

"Wow!" Bess said. "I didn't know Margaret was so pretty."

"I want to see if she's carrying a red purse," Nancy said, rushing ahead in Margaret's direction. "I'll see you guys later," she called over her shoulder.

Nancy wove her way through the crowd, nearly tripping over a pair of well-groomed Scottish terriers. "Hi," she said, catching up to Margaret. She smiled brightly. "Remember me?"

Margaret Parker frowned.

"I'm Nancy Drew," she reminded the assistant curator. "We met at Rapid Repair."

"Oh, right," Margaret replied, without enthusiasm.

"Did you ever find your earring?" Nancy asked, keeping up the conversation as they walked.

"No, I didn't," Margaret said coldly. Then, quickening her pace, she added, "If you'll excuse me, there's someone here I have to see."

79

Nancy's eyes followed the blond woman until she disappeared in the crowd. Margaret was not carrying a red purse, Nancy noted with disappointment, but a white one, which matched her shoes and hat.

Nancy turned toward the refreshment tent, trying to spot her friends, but Bess and George were nowhere in sight. She wandered over to the arena, where groups of dogs and their handlers were beginning to assemble. Nancy had never seen so many handsome dogs gathered at once.

Suddenly Su-Lin came up, holding two fierce-looking German shepherds on short leashes. "Nancy," she said. "How's your ankle?"

Nancy glanced down. "To tell you the truth, I'd forgotten all about it," she said. "That balm of yours must have really done the trick."

"The necklace looks great on you," Su-Lin said.

"I love wearing it," Nancy replied with a smile, touching the ornate silver locket.

Just then the German shepherds looked up at Nancy and growled. "Will the necklace protect me against wild beasts?" Nancy joked.

Su-Lin jerked the chain leashes. "Brutus! Caesar!" she said firmly. "Behave yourselves." The dogs licked their lips and eyed Nancy suspiciously.

"They look pretty fierce," Nancy remarked. "Are they yours?"

Su-Lin strained to hold the dogs back. "No, they belong to Professor Herbert," she said. She pointed out a tall, gray-haired man with a goatee who was talking to Margaret Parker. "I'm just looking after the dogs for him."

"Do you think you could introduce me to Professor Herbert?" Nancy asked.

"Sure," Su-Lin agreed. "But I have to get Brutus and Caesar over to the arena right now. Professor Herbert would be mortified if they missed out on the show. I was just taking them over to their handler."

"Okay, I'll catch up with you later," Nancy said. She waved to Su-Lin and headed toward the refreshment tent. It seemed the most likely place to find her friends.

Making her way through the crowd again, Nancy almost bumped into Nelson Stone. "Hello, Mr. Stone," Nancy said. The curator looked pale and tired, with beads of perspiration on his forehead.

"Nancy!" Nelson Stone cried, sounding pleased to see her. "I was hoping you'd be here. You know," he added in a confidential tone, "the police came to see me again." He pulled a handkerchief from his pocket and wiped his brow. "They don't seem to be making much progress finding the Golden Horse. And I don't think they're taking the threats on my life very seriously. All they did was ask me pointless questions," he complained.

"Actually," Nancy said, "I had a few things to ask you myself, Mr. Stone. Do you think we could—"

Just then a striking dark-haired woman cut into their conversation.

"Excuse me," she said to Nancy, "but your neck-

81

lace is *so* unusual." Her black eyes were fixed on Su-Lin's locket. "May I ask you where you got it?"

Out of the corner of her eye, Nancy noticed that Nelson Stone was also staring at the necklace. "Oh, a friend loaned it to me," Nancy answered vaguely.

Leaning forward, Stone said, "That's a Tibetan piece, I believe. A clerk at the museum has one just like it."

"Is it an antique?" asked the dark-haired woman.

Nancy shrugged uncomfortably. She wasn't happy with all the attention the necklace was attracting. But before Nancy had time to think of an answer, Nelson Stone said, "It must be very old, indeed. And quite valuable, I should think."

The woman's coal-black eyes glittered. "My husband, Justin Todd, is a jeweler," she told Nancy. "He makes wonderful antique reproductions." Turning, she beckoned to a blond, well-tanned man talking to Professor Herbert. "Justin!" she called. "Come over here and take a look at this."

The man frowned and stopped his conversation. "Just a moment, Fiona," he said.

Nelson Stone coughed. "I think I'd better rejoin the Museum Society trustees," he said, excusing himself. Then he added in a whisper to Nancy, "If it weren't for museum politics, I wouldn't have shown up today. I really dislike crowds." He nodded to Fiona, and as he departed, Justin Todd and Professor Herbert came forward.

"Justin, darling," Fiona said, waving a manicured

82

hand. "Do you think you could make me a copy of this lovely necklace?" Turning to Nancy, she added, "If you wouldn't mind, of course."

Justin Todd looked at the necklace and frowned. "I don't make copies," he said firmly.

"But, darling," Fiona insisted. "You make wonderful copies. What about that gorgeous——?"

Professor Herbert's face reddened. "Fiona," the professor said sharply, "you're embarrassing the young lady." Turning to Nancy, he said, "I'm Charles Herbert, and these are my friends, Justin and Fiona Todd."

"I'm Nancy Drew," she said, shaking hands.

Professor Herbert studied Nancy's face with sharp, gray eyes. "Would you be related to the attorney Carson Drew by any chance?"

Nancy nodded. "Yes, I'm his daughter."

"Ah," the professor said, rocking slightly on his heels. "Wasn't he Amanda Lane's attorney?"

"Yes, he was," Nancy replied.

"I'll bet he made a bundle handling her estate," Fiona Todd chimed in.

Justin Todd took his wife by the arm and said, "I think it's time we took a look at the dogs."

"So, you must be the famous teenage detective I've heard so much about," Professor Herbert said, turning back to Nancy.

"I'm not sure that I'm famous," Nancy said with a smile. "But I've solved a few mysteries here and there."

"I understand you were in the museum at the time of the robbery," Professor Herbert went on when the Todds were out of earshot.

"That's right," Nancy replied. "I met a student of yours, Su-Lin Tung, there. We've become good friends."

Professor Herbert's gaze lowered to Su-Lin's distinctive necklace. "Did she give that to you?" he asked.

Nancy clasped the locket. "Su-Lin loaned it to me," she told him.

Professor Herbert raised his eyebrows and pulled a leather tobacco pouch from his jacket pocket. "I'm surprised she'd loan such a valuable piece," he said, filling his pipe. "She told me once that she never opens the locket."

Nancy tried to change the subject. "Su-Lin mentioned that your specialty is Tibetan artifacts and that you've written a book on the subject."

Professor Herbert struck a match and drew on his pipe. "Yes, that's true," he said between puffs.

"I've become very interested in Tibet since meeting Su-Lin," Nancy went on. "Wasn't it just terrible that the Golden Horse was stolen?"

"Terrible," Professor Herbert echoed, stroking his neatly trimmed goatee. "I myself was particularly upset, since I was the one who encouraged the museum to make the purchase. In fact, I authenticated the piece for them."

"That's interesting," Nancy remarked. "Tell me,

Professor, do you think the museum paid too much for the Golden Horse?"

Professor Herbert arched an eyebrow. "What makes you ask that?" he said.

Nancy hesitated. "Oh, something Hillary Lane said the other day." She waited for his response to the heiress's name.

Professor Herbert leaned over and gave Nancy a wink. "Well, just between you and me, I wouldn't be surprised if Hillary Lane stole the Golden Horse herself. Mind you, now, I wouldn't want that remark to go beyond the two of us."

Nancy stared at him. "Why, how could anyone suspect Hillary?" she asked innocently.

"It should be obvious to a brilliant detective like yourself." The professor drew contentedly on his pipe. "It's no secret," he continued, his face disappearing behind a cloud of smoke, "that Hillary has been stewing ever since Stone outbid her at the auction."

At that moment a parade of fox terriers passed with their handlers, forcing Nancy and Professor Herbert to step aside.

Nancy remembered Hillary saying that she'd badly wanted the second Golden Horse for her collection. "Well," Nancy said finally, "I guess she wanted to see the pair reunited after all these years."

"Our Hillary is not so sentimental," Professor Herbert said with a smile. "There's something I'll bet she didn't tell you. The fact is, the value of the Golden

Horses would be multiplied several times over as a pair. They'd fetch a cool three million, at least."

Nancy considered the professor's words carefully. Was Hillary Lane greedy enough to steal the Golden Horse? Nancy was beginning to think it was a very real possibility.

9

Disaster at the Dog Show

Before Nancy could question Professor Herbert further about Hillary Lane, she heard George calling her name.

"Nancy!" George said breathlessly, running up. "Where have you been? The show is starting, and I can't find Bess. It's not like her to just disappear."

"Wasn't she with you?" Nancy asked in surprise.

Professor Herbert knocked the ashes from his pipe. "Well, I'd better run along now and check my dogs," he said. "It's been nice chatting with you, Nancy. If you're ever up at Westmoor University, feel free to drop by the anthropology department."

"I certainly will," Nancy said. "It was very nice meeting you."

"Who's the guy with the goatee?" George asked as the professor headed toward the arena.

"That's Professor Herbert from Westmoor," Nancy began, but she stopped when she saw Hillary Lane coming toward them.

"Hi there, Nancy," Hillary said. The heiress was dressed smartly in a short plaid skirt, a white silk blouse, and navy blazer. Hillary turned to George and extended a slim, graceful hand. "I'm Hillary Lane."

"Pleased to meet you," George said as they shook hands. "I'm George Fayne."

Hillary checked her gold watch. "The show should be starting any minute now," she said. She guided the girls toward the arena, where folding chairs were arranged in rows. "This is the best turnout we've ever had," Hillary went on. "With all these top pedigree dogs, it should be an interesting competition."

The heiress explained that there would be two parts to the show. "The first contest," she said, "is for best-in-breed. Then we'll have a short refreshment break, followed by the best-in-show competition."

At that moment one of the ushers rushed up to Hillary. "Ms. Lane," he said urgently. "The trainer for Mrs. Grimes's English sheepdog has taken ill. Mrs. Grimes is very upset."

"Oh, no!" Hillary frowned. "I hope it's not serious. What can we do on such short notice?"

"Well," the usher replied, "a young woman in the audience has volunteered to take the trainer's place."

Hillary glanced at him doubtfully. "But is she capable of handling the dog properly?" she asked.

"I've organized every detail of this show to perfection. I want this year's event to be really memorable."

The usher nodded. "The young woman does seem very confident. She says she's very experienced in walking dogs. And Mrs. Grimes is so eager to have Oliver shown."

Hillary sighed. "I guess that's the best we can do." As the man departed, Hillary said to the girls in a low voice, "I hope this girl knows what she's doing. Oliver can be quite a handful, as I remember."

The heiress pushed through the crowd, making a path for Nancy and George. "You'll have a good view from here," she said, leading them to seats near the judges' table. "I can't let Carson Drew's daughter sit in the back row." Hillary winked and hurried off.

A moment later Nancy realized that she and George were seated behind the Todds, who were whispering fiercely between themselves. Hearing her name mentioned, Nancy strained her ears. Unfortunately, the conversation was drowned out by the noisy chatter of the audience. Then a group of dalmatians began parading around the arena, and the audience quickly quieted down.

"Oh, Justin!" Nancy heard Fiona Todd snap. "You're being so difficult. Why can't you make me a copy of that necklace?"

"Obviously, darling, you don't understand," the blond man replied angrily. "I don't want everyone in town to know I copy antique jewelry. You should never have mentioned it in public."

"Oh, don't be ridiculous," Fiona chided. "There's

89

nothing wrong with making copies. That shop of yours might make more money if you specialized in reproductions, instead of that arty junk you design."

"Don't put down my jewelry shop," her husband hissed. "The Goldmine has been doing very well since we moved to the mall. Besides, I've only made one reproduction, and that was a special favor for Charles Herbert."

"That skinflint professor still owes you money on it, too," Fiona pointed out.

"Give the man a chance," Todd told his wife. "It's only been a month since I finished it. Anyway, Herbert told me in confidence that he's having some financial problems."

Just then George said to Nancy, "Hey, look! There's Bess."

"I don't believe it!" Nancy cried, clapping her hand to her mouth. "She's walking that English sheepdog!"

Suddenly Justin Todd turned around and saw Nancy seated behind him. His jaw dropped and his pale gray eyes narrowed. Obviously the jeweler realized that Nancy had overheard his conversation. Nancy looked straight ahead, pretending indifference.

George leaned over to Nancy. "What is Bess doing there? She's not a professional dog walker."

Nancy grinned. "Well, Bess does walk her neighbor's Scotty sometimes," she said. "This should be interesting."

Twenty minutes later Nancy and George were even more amazed when Oliver won first prize for best-in-breed. Bess graciously accepted the blue ribbon from the judge and handed it to a beaming Mrs. Grimes.

"One thing about your cousin," Nancy told George. "She sure can rise to an occasion." The two girls broke out in laughter.

During intermission the girls were eager to congratulate Bess.

"I thought I saw her heading this way," George said as they followed the crowd toward the refreshment tent. On the way Nancy noticed Professor Herbert huddled in conversation with Nelson Stone. Nudging George, she said, "Take a look over there."

"Those two don't seem to be getting on too well," George commented. "Look at the way the professor is glowering at Stone. It looks as if he's ready to drive him into the ground."

"And Stone looks pretty mad, too," Nancy observed. "Let's try to get a little closer."

But as the girls reached the tent, they heard a sudden shout, followed by a huge commotion around the refreshment table. All the sophisticated, smartly dressed people were now scattering in a frenzy.

Nancy looked over at the center of the confusion and spotted Bess struggling with the large sheepdog.

"Please, someone help me!" Bess cried. Juggling an ice cream cone in one hand, she was trying to pull the eager animal away from a wire garbage bin.

Nancy and George dashed to Bess's side. But by the time the three of them retrieved the dog from the bin, his beautifully groomed coat was covered in garbage.

"Oh, Oliver!" Bess cried. "How could you do this to me?"

"We'll never get all this muck out of his fur," George said, shaking her head as she held on tightly to the huge dog's collar.

Nancy ran over to a table and grabbed a handful of napkins. "Try these," she said, giving some to her friends.

"Maybe we'd better wash Oliver off at the duck pond," George finally suggested.

"We've got to get Oliver cleaned up quickly," Bess said as they dragged the sheepdog over to the duck pond. "The most important part of the show will be starting soon."

Nancy shook her head doubtfully. "I don't know, Bess," she said, watching George douse the dog with handfuls of water. "Oliver may have to bow out gracefully." The once-fluffy sheepdog was now a scrawny mess.

"Wow," Bess said. "I had no idea sheepdogs were so skinny underneath all that fur."

Suddenly the dog started to shake, spraying water everywhere. "Hey, watch out!" George warned, darting out of the way.

Bess jumped back and let go of the lead. "Oliver," she cried, "you're ruining my dress!"

As soon as the dog was free, he started running across the lawn. The three girls chased after him, but there was no hope of catching the dog before he dashed into the arena. There, in the middle of all the other dogs, he shook himself vigorously, spraying water in every direction.

People sitting in the first few rows scrambled out of Oliver's path. Dogs barked, and the judge called for everyone to calm down. Then Brutus, one of Professor Herbert's fierce German shepherds, nipped a French poodle in the back leg, and all havoc broke out.

Half an hour later the girls headed back to Nancy's car. "What a way to end a dog show," George said with a groan.

"Mrs. Grimes was really upset," Bess said somberly.

"Not as upset as Hillary Lane," George added.

"I'll say," Nancy remarked, but her mind was still on Nelson Stone. She was disappointed that she hadn't had a chance to talk to the curator alone.

"Well," George said, "Hillary did say she wanted the show to be memorable."

"It sure was," Nancy said, and they all laughed.

Just then the girls saw Hillary walking toward them from the parking area. Even from a few yards away, they could tell she was in a huff.

"I really should apologize again," Bess whispered to Nancy. But when the heiress spotted them, she turned off in another direction.

"She sure looks angry. Maybe I'll just write her a note," Bess said as they neared the blue Mustang.

Nancy frowned. Something about her car looked

odd. "Oh, no!" she cried. "Someone's smashed the window!"

Pulling the front door open, Nancy couldn't believe her eyes. On the driver's seat a note was pinned down with a long, sharp filleting knife. In bold letters, handprinted in red felt pen, the note read: Mind your own business, Nancy Drew!

10

Useful Evidence

"Who could have done such an awful thing?" Bess cried, looking over Nancy's shoulder.

Nancy took a piece of cardboard from the glove compartment and swept the glass off the front seat. Then she lifted the knife with a tissue and studied the sharp gash in the seat. "I don't know," she said, frowning.

"I'll bet it was Hillary Lane," George said. "We just saw her coming from the parking area, right?"

Nancy wrapped the knife in a scarf that had been lying on the back seat of the car. "Maybe the fingerprints on this knife will tell us something. I'll ask the police lab in River Heights to dust it."

"This whole business gives me the creeps," Bess

95

said, shuddering. She climbed into the backseat, watching for bits of glass.

Nancy stood for a moment, looking at the sun set behind the trees. Obviously, she had made someone nervous enough to try and scare her off the case. But the question was, who?

After driving her friends home, Nancy dropped the knife off at the River Heights police station lab. The officer at the desk told her that they were extremely busy, but that someone would contact Nancy soon with the results. There was nothing to do but wait.

That night Nancy couldn't sleep. Gazing out her bedroom window, she watched the moon rise in a starlit sky. An eerie feeling came over her as she considered who might have had an opportunity to leave the threatening note. She recalled Hillary Lane scowling as she left the parking area. Would the heiress have done such a nasty thing? Or maybe Margaret Parker had done it on her way out of the parking lot.

The next morning Nancy woke up determined to talk with Nelson Stone. It was time to get some straight answers.

The curator was in his office, talking on the phone, when Nancy arrived. He motioned her to come in. Covering the mouthpiece, he said, "Please have a seat. I'll be right off."

Nancy sat down in a leather chair. A few minutes later Stone put down the phone and turned to her. "Any breakthroughs yet?" he asked from behind his large mahogany desk. He picked up a letter opener and ran his index finger along the edge.

"Mr. Stone," Nancy began, her hands clasped calmly in her lap, "there are a few issues I need to clear up before I can continue with the case."

Stone arched a thick, dark eyebrow and touched his hawkish nose. "Oh, really?"

"Something has been troubling me," Nancy went on evenly. "Where were you last Thursday evening?"

Nelson Stone frowned. "I told you," he said. "I was watching 'Wheel of Chance' on TV."

"I don't think so," Nancy said, shaking her head. "Last Thursday 'Wheel of Chance' was canceled for the tennis tournament."

"Look, young lady," the curator said, rising angrily from his chair. "I don't need you to give me the TV listings." His dark, beady eyes took on a new boldness. "In fact, I don't need your detective services at all anymore."

"Oh?" Nancy said. "So you know now who sent you the threatening letter?"

Stone leaned forward, placing his palms squarely on the desk. "Everything's under control, thank you very much," he said.

Nancy hesitated. Should she reveal her suspicions about who she really thought had made the threats on Stone's life—Nelson Stone himself? She had a feeling his bravado was a cover-up. Beneath his words she sensed the curator was scared. There was no need to press him to come clean.

"Fine," Nancy said finally. "I'll just show myself

out." She left Stone's office and made her way through the marble corridor. Passing the Tibetan section, she glanced at the still-empty case and wondered if the Golden Horse would ever be returned to the museum. Somehow, she felt that there was still a chance she could do something to help.

In the hallway she passed a young man pinning a typed notice to the bulletin board. Suddenly it fell to the floor and skidded to her feet. As Nancy bent down to pick up the notice, Stone's distinctive signature caught her eye. But even more interesting, Nancy thought, was the fact that all the letter *t*'s had a distinctive break—just like the one in Stone's threatening letter. Silently Nancy handed the notice back to the young man.

Nancy hurried out of the building and returned to her car. Now she was sure that the letter sent to Stone had been typed on his own office typewriter. It wasn't absolute proof that Stone had typed it himself, of course. But she knew she was getting closer.

Half an hour later Nancy met George and Bess at Glad Rags in the mall. "Sorry I'm late," she told George, who was standing outside the dressing room.

George gave a weary shrug. "You didn't miss anything," she told her. "Bess has spent the last hour trying to find the perfect dress for her cousin's wedding."

"Has she had any luck?" Nancy asked, checking her hair in the mirror.

"Not exactly." George chuckled. "She's looking for a dress that makes her look two sizes smaller."

Just then the dressing room door swung open and Bess emerged, wearing a flowing, pink silk dress. "I love it!" she said, twirling around. "It's exactly what I wanted."

Nancy and George nodded their enthusiasm. It wasn't long before the dress was wrapped and the girls were deciding where to have lunch.

"Let's try the Black Swan for a change," Nancy suggested. "We haven't been there in ages."

"Yuck." Bess wrinkled her nose in distaste. "They serve those tiny, dried-up sandwiches."

"I have a good reason," Nancy told her with a grin. "I want to stake out the jewelry shop across from it."

"Does this, by any chance, have anything to do with the Stone case?" George asked as they walked across the mall.

"It could," Nancy said, spotting a window seat in the busy restaurant. Over lunch she filled her friends in on her meeting with Nelson Stone and the notice that had fallen in her path.

George slapped the table. "Stone must have written the letter!" she exclaimed.

"Wait a minute," Bess said. "Margaret Parker could easily have used Stone's typewriter. She probably types all of his letters."

"That's true," Nancy agreed. "But Stone seems the most likely suspect. He did send the chocolates to himself, and I've already caught him in a lie about his whereabouts on Thursday night."

Nancy glanced out the window at the Goldmine jewelry shop. A young couple was looking at wedding rings in the window. But she could see, through the glass door, that the shop didn't seem very busy.

"You still haven't told us why you're keeping an eye on the Goldmine," Bess reminded Nancy.

"It's a long shot," Nancy said. "To tell you the truth, I'm not sure what I'll find there."

Just then she saw Justin Todd leave the store. Grabbing the check, she said, "This is my treat, okay? Come on, let's pay a visit to the Goldmine."

George and Bess exchanged confused looks as Nancy paid the bill.

"Listen," Nancy said quickly as they crossed the mall, "I want you guys to chat with the salesman. Tell him you're going to take a course in jewelry design—that you want to see how the stuff is made, or something. I want to get a look around their workshop."

A bell jingled when the girls entered the Goldmine. Nancy quickly tucked Su-Lin's necklace under her knit pullover. She didn't want to draw extra attention to it.

"May I help you?" the blond salesman asked from behind a glass showcase. Nancy wondered if he might be Justin's younger brother.

"Is it all right if we browse?" Nancy asked. "We're trying to get ideas for a gift."

"Of course," he said, flashing a friendly smile. "There's plenty to choose from. Everything you see here is made in our workshop."

"Oh, is your workshop on the premises?" Nancy asked.

"That's right," the salesman replied. "Mr. Todd is a master craftsman. His designs are quite unique."

"Oh, how interesting," George gushed. "I'd like to be a jewelry designer myself someday. In fact, I'm starting a jewelry course next week," she fibbed.

"Then you'll probably have a special appreciation for Mr. Todd's work," the salesman said. He slid open the showcase and pulled out a tray of silver and enamel bracelets. "These are some of his latest designs."

"Wow!" George said. "Are they baked in a kiln?"

The young man nodded.

Bess joined in. "That's how they finish pottery, right?"

Nancy pointed to a pair of silver bookends. "How do you make those?" she asked.

"Oh, the swans," the salesman said. "They're one of my favorite pieces. Very unusual." He took the bookends down from the shelf. "We melt the silver in a small electric furnace before pouring it into a mold," he explained.

George sighed. "I've never seen anything like that. I'd love to know more about the process."

"So would I," Nancy added.

The salesman scratched his chin. "Well, Mr. Todd doesn't usually allow people into the workshop," he said slowly.

"Oh, please," Bess cajoled. "Just a quick peek. We promise not to disturb anything."

The salesman glanced at his watch. "Sure, why

not?" he said finally. "Mr. Todd won't be back for another half hour."

The girls followed him into the workshop at the back of the store. It was a small room with a cluttered workbench running along one side. Photographs and drawings of jewelry designs were pinned on the wall above the bench.

The salesman pointed out the furnace and the kiln at the far end of the workbench. Then, climbing a stepladder, he reached for a metal object on a high shelf. "The molds are kept up here," he explained. "We used this one to make the swans." He stepped down from the ladder and showed the girls a heavy metal mold.

Just then there was another jingle from the shop door.

"I'll be right back," the young man said, placing the mold down on the workbench.

As soon as he had disappeared, Nancy whispered, "Quick! Hold the stepladder for me. I want to get up there."

George and Bess steadied the ladder as Nancy scrambled up and grabbed hold of the top shelf.

"What is she doing up there?" Bess asked, flashing George a worried look.

George shrugged. "I don't know," she whispered. "But she'd better get down fast before that guy comes back."

Suddenly Nancy heard the salesman shout, *"Hey!* What are you doing up there?"

George and Bess jumped back in surprise, and

Nancy looked down. In the next second she felt the ladder wobble beneath her feet. Her stomach knotted in fear as all at once she lost her balance. The ladder toppled over, leaving Nancy hanging from the shelf.

"Get down from there!" the young man yelled. Nancy gripped the shelf with all her might. Suddenly it began to bend under her weight. Then, with a loud crack, the wooden shelf broke in half! Nancy fell to the floor, followed by splintered pieces of shelf. Molds showered down around her, as she shielded her head with her arms.

"Look what you've done!" the salesman cried. "This will cost me my job!"

But as Nancy struggled to get up, she spotted what she'd been looking for. On the floor beside her was a metal mold in the shape of the Golden Horse!

11

A Visit with Professor Herbert

"What were you looking for back there?" George asked Nancy as the girls scrambled into the car a few minutes later.

"Yeah, why were you climbing those shelves?" Bess asked from the backseat. "That poor salesman . . . Well, we did offer to clean up."

Nancy related the conversation she'd overheard at the dog show between Fiona and Justin Todd. "Fiona was trying to get her husband to make her a copy of Su-Lin's necklace," Nancy began. "She reminded Justin that he'd copied an antique for Professor Herbert. Obviously it was some kind of secret, because Justin was furious with Fiona for blabbing about it in public."

"Wait a minute," George said, frowning. "I was sitting right there, and I didn't hear a thing."

"Nancy's ears are highly tuned to that kind of stuff," Bess teased.

Nancy braked for a red light. "Well, I think that antique Todd made for Herbert was a copy of the Golden Horse," she said. "I couldn't be certain, though, until I saw the mold," she said. "But the timing tipped me off. Todd made the copy about a month ago. That was about the time that Professor Herbert appraised the Golden Horse for the museum." The light changed, and Nancy accelerated across the intersection.

"The professor has a special interest in the Golden Horses," she went on. "Su-Lin told me he devoted a whole chapter to them in his book. Anyway, Herbert knew his friend Todd had the know-how to copy the piece, so it was easy to imagine he might ask him to do the favor."

"What's wrong with having a copy made?" Bess asked.

"Nothing, really," George said. "Plenty of people own copies of fine art, right?"

"There's nothing wrong with owning a copy, but Justin Todd's secrecy makes me suspicious," Nancy said.

George chewed her lip thoughtfully. "Maybe Stone found out that Herbert had the horse copied, and that's why they were arguing at the dog show," she suggested.

"That's a thought," Nancy said, fingering the Tibet-an necklace Su-Lin had given her.

"Too bad we weren't able to overhear Stone and Herbert arguing," George said.

"I wonder if we can use this situation to our advantage," Nancy said slowly. "Maybe I could get Herbert to talk about Stone. He might let some kind of useful information slip out."

Nancy checked her watch. It was only two o'clock. "How about a drive out to Westmoor University?" she asked her friends.

"I'd love to," George said, "but I think Bess has a dental appointment in half an hour."

"Did you have to remind me?" Bess said as Nancy made a right and headed toward the River Heights Medical Center.

"See you guys later," Bess said with a sigh, stepping out of the car as they pulled up. "I'll take a cab home."

After dropping Bess off, Nancy drove out to Westmoor University with George. A short while later they were walking across the sprawling campus. George stopped a student and asked for directions to the anthropology department.

"It's in Harris Hall," the young woman said, point-ing to a large brick building across the lawn.

The girls headed toward the building and entered through the large front doors. They found a directory posted in the lobby. Professor Herbert's office was on the third floor.

"I guess it'd be better if you went up alone," George suggested. "I'll take a walk around the campus."

Nancy agreed to meet George back in the lobby in half an hour. She entered the elevator and pressed the button for the third floor, hoping the professor would be available.

When the doors opened, Nancy was surprised to see Su-Lin in a crowd of students down the hall. "Su-Lin!" she called, stepping off the elevator.

Su-Lin waved as she made her way through the crowd. "Nancy," she said, flashing a smile. "What a nice surprise."

"I just came by with a friend," Nancy explained breezily. "I thought I'd stop and have a chat with Professor Herbert. I did get to meet him at the dog show, after all."

Su-Lin glanced at the wall clock. "He's lecturing right now, I think," she said, adjusting her book bag over her shoulder. "But he should be back in his office soon. Why don't you have a soda with me in the student lounge while you're waiting?"

"Sounds great," Nancy said. Su-Lin led her down the hall to a large, sunny room furnished with leather chairs and couches. The girls got sodas from the vending machine, then found comfortable seats in the corner. Their conversation soon turned to Nelson Stone. Nancy wanted to know more about his relationship with Herbert.

"I think Mr. Stone has great respect for the professor professionally," Su-Lin said. "He did ask him to appraise the Golden Horse, you know. But I wouldn't call them friends, exactly."

"Who are Stone's friends?" Nancy asked. "Do you have any idea?"

Su-Lin shrugged. "He's been too busy stepping on toes to make friends, I guess," she said.

Nancy nodded. "I gathered that he wasn't winning any popularity contests." Then, lowering her voice, she said, "Listen, Su-Lin. Stone kicked me off his case. But I may be onto something else—something that might lead to the Golden Horse. It's a real long shot, so I can't go into details. But right now I need your help more than ever. I'd like you to keep your eyes and ears open at the museum for anything that seems at all unusual."

"I sure will," Su-Lin promised. "I do hope you'll be able to find the Golden Horse."

Nancy said goodbye to Su-Lin and sent regards to her father. Then she walked down the hall to Professor Herbert's office.

The secretary looked up from her typing as Nancy entered. "May I help you?" she asked.

"Is Professor Herbert in?" Nancy asked.

"He's on the phone right now," the secretary said. She nodded toward the professor's inner office, where the door had been left ajar. "Have a seat while you wait."

Nancy sat down in an oak chair as the secretary continued typing. A few moments later the woman stopped abruptly, muttering something as she changed the typewriter cassette ribbon. Then the phone rang.

"Hello, Dr.—I mean Professor Herbert's office," the secretary answered. "He's on another line. Would you like to hold?" She pressed a button on the console, hung up, and turned to Nancy. "This is my first day on the job," she confided.

Suddenly the intercom buzzer sounded and the secretary picked up the phone again. "Oh, Professor Herbert, there's a Mr. Sharp on line two." Then she turned back to Nancy. "I'm sure he'll be free in just a few minutes."

As the secretary returned to her typing, Nancy got up and wandered over to the window. She could hear Professor Herbert's voice drifting through the partly opened door. Nancy strained her ears against the clatter of the typewriter to pick out the words of his conversation.

"Of course we agree on the price," she heard him say. "I'll have my secretary type up all the details for your client. I'm sure he'll be pleased. As you know, it's a very rare piece."

Nancy's pulse quickened. Was Professor Herbert trying to sell Todd's copy of the Golden Horse? She tried to hear more, but the shrill sound of the ringing telephone drowned out Herbert's voice.

Nancy returned to her chair just as Herbert appeared at the door. He was holding a stack of papers, which he gave to the secretary. Then he noticed

Nancy and smiled broadly. "Well, well," he said, extending his hand. "What a surprise to see you again."

Nancy stood up and shook his hand. "I was on campus, and I thought I'd just drop in."

"Glad you did," the professor said, ushering her into his office. It was a large, wood-paneled room filled with the scent of pipe tobacco. A colorful, hand-woven rug covered most of the floor, and the walls were completely lined with books.

Nancy took a seat as the professor lowered himself into a swivel chair behind his desk.

"Excuse all this clutter," he said, waving a hand in front of him. "My last secretary used to keep things neater. Anyway, tell me—how is River Heights' famous teenage detective doing?" he asked with a chuckle.

Nancy sensed that Professor Herbert didn't take her very seriously. She decided to use that to her advantage. "Not very well," she said. "I haven't had any new cases lately. In fact, I was thinking of signing up for some anthropology courses here at Westmoor."

Herbert leaned back in his chair and stroked his goatee thoughtfully. "I can't think of a more interesting field," he said finally. "I've been fascinated by it for the last thirty years." Then, leaning forward, his eyes fixed on the Tibetan necklace around Nancy's neck. "I must say, that's a remarkable piece," he said. "You know, it's a Tibetan tradition for a groom to give such a necklace as a wedding gift. Often amulets are

110

kept inside—or in some cases, precious stones, like rubies or diamonds."

Nancy put her hand to the silver locket. "That's very interesting," she said.

"I've often wondered what was inside Su-Lin's locket," Herbert said. "She's always been so secretive about it that I sense it must be something of great value. If you don't mind my asking—have you ever taken a peek?"

"No," Nancy replied flatly, hoping to put an end to his questions. "Su-Lin asked me not to." Too late, she realized that her words only added to his curiosity.

Just then there was a knock at the door. "Come in," Professor Herbert called. His secretary entered and handed him some typed pages.

"Here are those papers on the Golden Horse," she said.

Herbert flashed the secretary an annoyed look, and Nancy's suspicions began to mount. Maybe the professor *was* trying to sell a copy of the Golden Horse to this Mr. Sharp. "Well, I guess I'd better be off," Nancy said, standing up. "My friend is waiting for me downstairs."

"Always a pleasure," Herbert said, rising to shake her hand. "Let me know if you decide to take those classes. Maybe I can be of help."

Nancy thanked him, then left the room, closing the door behind her. Passing the secretary's desk, she glanced at the typewriter, wondering what was in the documents the woman had just typed. Was Professor

111

Herbert trying to pass off his copy of the Golden Horse as the real thing?

Keeping one eye on Herbert's office door, Nancy leaned over the desk and flipped up the lid of the typewriter. Then she snapped out the cassette ribbon and tucked it into her bag.

Quickly Nancy moved around the desk, opened the top drawer, and looked for a new cassette to replace the one she'd taken. Suddenly she heard footsteps as the doorknob turned. Nancy slammed the drawer shut, hurried out of the office, and flew down the steps of the stairwell.

She found George soaking up the sunshine on the front steps of Harris Hall. "Hurry!" Nancy urged. "We've got to get out of here right away."

"What else is new?" George quipped. "Don't tell me you pulled down some more shelves."

"This isn't a time to joke," Nancy said, running with George across the campus to the parking lot. "I had to steal some evidence, and I didn't have time to cover my tracks."

It wasn't until Nancy was driving off campus and had had a chance to catch her breath that she explained to her friend what had happened.

"It sounds like you're really onto something," George said.

Nancy tightened her grip on the wheel. "Let's hope so," she said. "We'll find out more when I decipher the tape. I should be able to figure out the words, letter by letter. But right now I'm pretty worried about the secretary finding that cassette gone. Rats!"

she cried in frustration. "I didn't have time to find another cartridge."

About two miles from the college campus Nancy glanced in her rearview mirror. "You see that tan car behind us, George? It's been following us ever since we left Westmoor."

George craned her neck. "Who do you think it is?" she asked, squinting.

Just then a black van with dark tinted windows overtook the tan car and roared up alongside them.

"Watch out!" George cried as the van veered closer. "He's trying to knock us off the road!"

Nancy twisted the wheel and stamped hard on the brakes. But the van continued to force her closer to the edge.

For a long moment Nancy fought desperately to keep the car on the road. But it was no use. The Mustang was about to plunge down the side of the ravine!

12

The Plot Thickens

"Hold on!" Nancy cried. The front end of the car turned over the cliff and began to slide down the ravine.

Suddenly the Mustang hit a dense clump of bushes and came to a standstill. Badly shaken, Nancy slowly struggled out of the car. "Are you all right?" she asked her friend.

George examined a scrape on her arm. "Whew! That was close. We could have been killed."

Nancy gazed into the distance, where the side of the ravine was much steeper. "If this little accident had happened farther along the road," she said, "we wouldn't have had a chance."

"It's lucky we didn't hit a tree, too," George said, stepping out of the car.

"Someone is definitely trying to keep us off this case," Nancy said, inspecting a dent on the car's radiator grill.

It wasn't long before they heard the sound of approaching police sirens. A few minutes later two local policemen came down the ravine, followed by two paramedics.

"We're over here," Nancy called.

"Is anyone hurt?" an officer called back.

"Just a few scratches and bruises," Nancy replied. "But we're sure glad to see you." She quickly related the details of the accident to the police.

As a paramedic administered first aid to George's scraped arm, an officer walked around to the front of Nancy's Mustang. "You girls got off lightly," he said.

The other officer shook his head. "If it hadn't been for this thicket of bushes, I figure it could have been much worse." Suddenly his hand-held radio squawked a message, and he unhooked it from his belt. "Yes, we're sending the ambulance back," he said into the radio. "No one's seriously hurt. But we need a tow truck here to get the car out of the ravine."

The girls followed the rescue team back up the ravine. "You sure got here fast," Nancy remarked to the officers. "We could have been stuck down here for hours."

"Yeah," the officer replied. "You were lucky the lady driving behind you had a car phone. She called nine-one-one and reported the accident."

"Did she get a license plate number of the van that hit us?" Nancy asked.

"She's giving one of our men a statement now," the officer said.

"There she is," a paramedic said. He pointed to a blond woman who was standing on the roadside, talking to a policeman. "She's the person you have to thank."

Nancy grabbed George by the arm. "Hey, that looks like Margaret Parker!" she exclaimed, stopping suddenly. "She must have been driving the tan car that was following us."

"That's weird," George said.

"Very weird," Nancy agreed as they continued up the ravine. "I want to talk to her. And not just to say thanks for making a phone call."

Nancy saw the policeman hand Margaret a clipboard, and she reluctantly scribbled something on it.

Nearing the top of the ravine, Nancy called, "Margaret!"

The blond woman turned on her heels and hurried toward her car. Nancy struggled up the steep incline, but by the time she reached the road, the tan car was already pulling out.

"I guess Margaret didn't want to answer any questions," George said, catching up to Nancy.

"Like why she was following us, for starters," Nancy replied grimly.

"Hey!" George said, snapping her fingers. "I've seen that tan car before."

"There are lots of tan cars around," Nancy said.

"But not one with a sticker that says Visualize World Peace," George pointed out. "That was the same tan car I saw leaving the museum on the day of the robbery."

"You're sure about that?" Nancy asked.

"Absolutely," George replied.

"Then it's almost certain that Margaret was at the museum when the Golden Horse was stolen," Nancy said.

A few moments later the tow truck arrived. As it pulled the Mustang from the ravine, Nancy filled out a report on the accident. Flipping to the previous page, she glanced at Margaret's report and noted the young woman's Clinton Park address.

An hour later, as dusk began to fall, Nancy and George drove up to Margaret Parker's small white house.

"She can't be too terrible a person," George said. "After all, she did report the accident."

"That's true," Nancy replied. "But I'd like to know why she was following us and then ran away." Even more, Nancy added to herself, I'd like to know why she insisted she wasn't at the museum on the day of the robbery.

As the girls walked up the driveway, Nancy dug into her bag, found the gold earring, and tucked it into her skirt pocket. Then, reaching the front door, she rang the buzzer.

"No one seems to be answering," George said after a few moments. She went around to the driveway. "Her car's here," she called out.

Nancy buzzed again. Then, lifting the letter slot, she called through the door, "Margaret, it's Nancy Drew! Please open up. I'd like to talk to you."

A few moments of silence passed. The girls exchanged glances.

"Margaret," Nancy tried again. "I know you're in there. And I know you must be frightened, or you wouldn't be hiding like this."

Suddenly the door flew open. "I'm not afraid of *anything*," Margaret snapped, her arms folded tightly across her chest.

"Then I'm sure you won't mind if we came in for a few minutes," Nancy told her. "I'd like to give you a chance to clear something up."

Margaret's lips tightened. "There's nothing to clear up," she said. "I saw your car go over the edge of the ravine, and I called the police. That's all there is to it. I've already made a statement to the police."

"Did you also tell the police that you were following us?" Nancy asked.

The color drained from Margaret's face. "That's ridiculous," she said. "I wasn't following you."

"Right," Nancy retorted, "just like you weren't at the museum on the day of the robbery."

George stepped forward and looked straight at Margaret. "I saw your car leave the museum a few minutes after the robbery," she said evenly. "I'm willing to testify to it."

118

Margaret looked from Nancy to George, her lower lip trembling slightly.

Nancy produced the gold earring from her pocket. "Does this look familiar?" she asked. "I believe you lost it near a window on the second floor of the museum on the day of the robbery."

Margaret lunged for the earring.

Nancy clenched her fist around the gold earring and returned it to her pocket. "I think we'd better talk, Margaret," she said.

With a heavy sigh the young woman turned, and the girls followed her into the house. Moving through the hallway, Nancy noticed a red leather purse on the telephone table. This time she was certain it was the same purse she had seen on a chair in Margaret's office, just before the Golden Horse was stolen.

They entered a small, comfortably furnished living room, and the girls seated themselves on the couch. Margaret sat across from them on a blue velvet chair and crossed her legs. "You can't prove anything, Nancy Drew," she said, studying her nails.

"You'd be surprised what I can prove," Nancy said, bluffing. "Not only can I prove you stole the Golden Horse—I can prove you cut Stone's brake pipes and sent him poisoned chocolates. That's attempted murder."

Margaret gasped in horror. "You've got it wrong!" she insisted. "I didn't do all of those things." She looked confused.

"It's the police you'll have to convince," Nancy

said, continuing to bluff. "Attempted murder is a very serious crime."

Margaret hid her face in her hands. "Oh, no! This has gone too far," she sobbed. "I told him I didn't want to get involved. But he said my job depended on it. He made me promises. He said he'd help me in my career."

"Who did?" Nancy pressed.

Margaret slumped back in her chair and sighed. "Mr. Stone. It was all his idea to . . ." She shook her head, as if she couldn't bear to say the words.

"To what?" Nancy persisted. "Steal the Golden Horse?"

Margaret shook her head again. "It wasn't the *real* Golden Horse that I stole. It was a fake."

"You mean," George blurted, "the museum's statue was actually a fake?"

"Yes," Margaret whispered.

"But how could that be?" George said, frowning. "The museum just paid over a million dollars for it."

"I know, I know," Margaret said. "It was a ridiculous mistake. Believe me, Mr. Stone thought he was getting the genuine article. It was authenticated by an expert."

"Professor Herbert?" Nancy asked.

"Right," Margaret replied with a nod. "But then, a month later, Mr. Stone showed the statue to a visiting Tibetan anthropologist, who recognized it as a fake. We took it somewhere else for another carbon dating. And sure enough, it was a recent copy."

"Why didn't you complain to the person who sold it to you?" George asked.

"It was a foreign dealer who skipped town," Margaret explained. "He was using a phony name, too."

"Then why not go back to Herbert?" Nancy asked.

"The publicity would have been awful," Margaret said. "Besides, we couldn't blame Herbert. He had only given a professional opinion. It was our responsibility to make the final decision. It would have destroyed Stone's professional reputation. And my own career would be ruined. All my life I've wanted to be a museum curator."

"So you figured you'd steal the fake to get rid of the evidence," Nancy said. "And the museum would get its money back from the insurance company. Everything would be neat and tidy, and no one would ever know about Stone's big mistake."

Margaret nodded. She seemed relieved the truth was out.

"So Nelson Stone definitely wrote the threatening letter to himself," Nancy continued. "He wanted me to be there in his office when the robbery took place. It gave him a perfect alibi, because he knew that the police would believe me. All you had to do was wait in your office until I passed by with Mr. Stone. Then you took the statue and made your exit through the fire escape."

Margaret nodded again.

"Stone thought he'd keep me busy with those bogus attempts on his life," Nancy went on. "I can't believe he'd actually sever the brake line on his own car. He put himself in serious danger doing that. And when he realized I was getting too close, he had you keep an eye on me. Tell me, Margaret," Nancy asked, "did Stone intentionally try to poison that poor dog?"

The blond woman looked as if she were going to cry again. "I'm afraid so. Mr. Stone got carried away, trying to make the threats on his life look real. He's the one who pushed you into the toolshed, too, to get the hacksaw. And he smashed the window in your car and left the note."

"I'm sorry," Nancy said, "but we'll have to report this to the police. If you tell them the truth, they may go easier on you."

Margaret nodded glumly as Nancy went to the hallway and phoned the police.

After Nancy hung up the phone, Margaret came into the hallway, holding a golden statue of a horse. "This is what I took from the museum," she said, handing the piece to Nancy.

George moved forward and took a closer look. "I've never seen the original," she said, "but it sure looks real to me."

A short while later the doorbell rang, and Nancy led Lieutenant Higgins and Officer Jenkins into the house.

"Well, well," Lieutenant Higgins said, entering the living room. "If it isn't Nancy Drew. McGinnis told me you were good." He stepped forward, eyeing the statue. "So this is the famous Golden Horse, huh?" he said. "The insurance company will be very glad to hear that it has been recovered, I'm sure."

Nancy smiled as she handed the statue over. "I don't think so, Lieutenant. I'm afraid this one's a fake."

Lieutenant Higgins did a double take, and Nancy repeated Margaret's story.

"Okay," he said. "We'll take over from here." He thanked Nancy for her help, then turned to Margaret. Nancy decided that it was time for her and George to leave.

"There's one thing I'm not clear on," George said as they got back in the car. "Herbert had the jeweler make him a copy of the Golden Horse, but did Herbert ever have the real one to copy?"

"Good question," Nancy said. "Either the professor really did make a mistake and authenticated a fake—or he switched horses at the time of the appraisal and gave Todd's copy back to the museum."

George whistled softly.

"So that means," Nancy said, "that Professor Herbert may have the *real* Golden Horse!"

13

Risky Business

"Don't worry," Nancy said to George, starting up her car. "I may have a way to find out if Professor Herbert has the real Golden Horse." Pulling out from behind the police car, she added grimly, "If he hasn't sold it already."

"That would be terrible," George said as they turned onto the main road.

Just then a vintage Cadillac swung past them, heading in the opposite direction.

"Hey!" Nancy cried. "That's Stone!"

"He must be going to Margaret Parker's place," George said.

Nancy made a quick U-turn and followed the

Cadillac. "Well, he's in for a big surprise when he sees Lieutenant Higgins."

A moment later the girls saw Stone's car slow down in front of the assistant curator's house. Then, suddenly, the Cadillac accelerated with a screech of tires.

"He saw the police car," Nancy said. "But he won't escape that way. It's a dead end."

At the far end of the road Stone made a rapid three-point turn, then came roaring back down the road.

"Here he comes!" George exclaimed.

Nancy swung her Mustang around, blocking Stone's escape. There was a sudden scream of tires against the asphalt, and smoke billowed out from the wheels as Stone's car skidded toward them.

"Watch out!" George cried. "He's going to hit us!"

A few feet away from Nancy's car the Cadillac finally careened to a halt. For a brief moment Nelson Stone stared at them with frightened eyes. Then he opened the door and jumped out of his car. "Get out of my way!" he yelled, waving a fist.

"Quick! Close your window," Nancy said to George, flicking a switch to lock the doors. She put her hand on the horn and held it there. Through the rearview mirror, she saw Lieutenant Higgins running toward them.

Stone turned and was about to run when Lieutenant Higgins shouted, "Stop right there!"

Nancy and George jumped out of the car as the police officer ran up to Stone.

"What is all this about?" Stone demanded.

Lieutenant Higgins took a pair of handcuffs from his belt and snapped them on Stone's wrists. "I'm arresting you for conspiracy with Margaret Parker in the theft of the Golden Horse and attempted insurance fraud." He began to read the curator his rights.

"Margaret Parker's a dirty liar," Stone protested.

"We'll let the judge decide that," Lieutenant Higgins said, leading Stone toward the police car. Then, turning to Nancy, the lieutenant added, "Good work, Nancy. We have a full confession from Margaret Parker."

Officer Jenkins came out of the house with Margaret and put her in the backseat of the police car, next to Stone.

As the police car roared away, George said, "Well, I guess that wraps things up."

"I wish it did," Nancy replied. "But I'm afraid we have our work cut out for us."

A short while later the girls returned to Nancy's house. As soon as they reached her room, Nancy pulled the typewriter cassette from her bag. "I'm hoping this will tell us what Professor Herbert is up to," she told George.

For the next ten minutes Nancy stretched the cassette ribbon under a light, trying to decipher the words, while George jotted them down on a notepad.

"A lot of this is too blurred to make out," Nancy said, disappointed.

A few minutes later, however, the sentences started to string together. "This is it!" George cried. She looked down at her notepad and whistled softly. "It looks as if the professor is claiming he has the genuine article," she said. "He's trying to sell the statue to that Sharp guy you told me about."

"I wish there was a way to intercept the deal," Nancy said, half to herself. Sharp's address on the tape was completely unreadable.

"I guess all you can do now," George said, "is take the cassette to the police."

Nancy shook her head. "No way. They'd never believe it. I'd need a copy of that letter. I want to search Herbert's office tonight."

"What's this *I* stuff all about?" George blurted. "You're not going without me, are you?"

Nancy hesitated and looked at her friend. "This might be risky, George . . ."

"Give me a break," George replied. "When did a little danger ever scare me off? You and I have been in plenty of tight spots together."

Nancy grinned. "Okay, but don't say I didn't warn you."

Nancy searched in her desk drawer and found her lock-picking kit. Then she went to her closet and pulled out some dark clothes. Both girls changed into black tops and jeans. Nancy tied her hair into a tight ponytail and pulled on a navy ski cap. Thin, black leather gloves completed her outfit.

"We look like a couple of cat burglars," George quipped.

Nancy inspected herself in the mirror, and her eyes fixed on Su-Lin's jade necklace. She put her hand to the silver locket and tucked it under her sweatshirt. If I ever needed luck, she told herself, it's tonight.

By ten o'clock Nancy and George were on the Westmoor University campus, which was quiet and mostly deserted, except for a few students entering the campus coffeehouse. Walking quickly toward Harris Hall, the girls found a side service door open. They crept softly up the stairwell to the anthropology department on the third floor. Nancy stopped and turned to George. "You stay here and keep a look out, okay? Don't forget to keep one eye on the elevator down the hall."

Nancy hurried down the dimly lit corridor until she reached the door to Herbert's office. For a moment she stood still, listening. The heavy silence and sweet smell of waxed woodwork gave her a heady feeling.

She took a deep breath and forced down the nervous fluttering in her stomach. Then she expertly inserted one of her lock-picks into the lock and turned it carefully.

Suddenly George came running down the corridor. "Quick!" she said. "The elevator's coming up!"

Silently the girls slipped inside the outer office, then waited breathlessly as the elevator passed the third floor and rumbled up the shaft.

Closing the door behind them, Nancy moved past the secretary's desk and into Herbert's office. She switched on the shaded desk light, then turned to George. "Let's start with the file cabinets," she whispered. "Look under S for Sharp."

It wasn't long before the two of them had exhausted all possibilities in the file cabinets. Nancy moved over to the professor's desk and tried the top drawer. It was locked. Suddenly they heard a scraping sound in the outside office.

Both girls froze. "Hurry!" Nancy called to George. "Behind the couch!"

But before Nancy had a chance to hide, a large, heavyset woman entered the office, carrying a vacuum cleaner.

Nancy pulled off her cap, so that she wouldn't look like a burglar, and stuffed it into her back pocket. Then she slipped off her gloves and dropped them behind a chair.

At that moment the woman reached over and flicked on the light switch, illuminating the room.

Nancy forced a smile. "Hello," she said casually. She pretended to be reading through a file on Herbert's desk.

The woman lumbered forward. "You're going to ruin your eyes in that light," she scolded. "So the professor's got you working overtime, eh? That's why his last secretary quit. What's your name, dear?"

"Name?" Nancy stalled, trying to compose herself. "Oh—Bess," she finally blurted, hoping George wouldn't let out a giggle from behind the couch.

"I'm Mrs. Hopper," the woman said. She leaned toward Nancy conspiratorially. "And if you don't mind my giving you a little advice—don't let that Professor Herbert bully you into working such late hours."

Nancy lowered her eyes. "Actually, I just came by to photocopy some important papers that have to be sent out," she said. "I forgot to do it this afternoon. But now I can't find them." She pulled on the drawer, then shrugged. "I guess the professor locked them up."

The woman winked. "Maybe I can help," she said. The next minute Mrs. Hopper was on her knees, groping under the desk. "Here it is," she said, handing over a small brass key. "I knew I'd seen a spare taped under here."

"Thanks," Nancy said, peeling away the cellophane tape. She inserted the key into the lock and quickly pulled open the desk drawer. Out of the corner of her eye she saw Mrs. Hopper cross the room and head toward the couch, dragging the vacuum cleaner behind her. A few more feet and she was bound to spot George.

"Mrs. Hopper!" Nancy called. "Please—could you come back later?"

The cleaning woman stared at her blankly.

"I mean, after I've finished," Nancy continued. "I'll only be a few minutes. You see, I have to concentrate, and I don't want to be in your way."

Mrs. Hopper checked her pocket watch. "Oh, all right," she said. "I suppose I can start on Professor Mathew's office upstairs."

Nancy breathed a sigh of relief as Mrs. Hopper turned and waddled out of the office.

Once the woman was out of earshot, Nancy called to George. It wasn't long before they had found a carbon copy of Herbert's letter to Sharp in the top drawer.

"Bingo!" Nancy cried. "Exactly what we need. The police will have to believe this. It's right here in black and white. Look—Herbert claims he has the authentic Golden Horse. And he's selling it for five hundred thousand dollars. That's half its value. I guess stolen goods don't go for the full price."

"It still looks like he's making Sharp a deal he can't refuse," George said.

"I wonder if Sharp knows the statue is stolen," Nancy mused.

"Let's make a copy of the letter," George suggested, "and then we're out of here."

Just then they heard a low snarling growl in the outer office.

George grabbed Nancy's arm. "That's not the cleaning woman," she said.

"Oh, no!" Nancy cried. She'd just spotted two snarling German shepherds in the doorway—and they were headed straight toward them!

14

A Desperate Struggle

Nancy quickly stuffed the letter in her pocket, then grabbed a chair to fend off the German shepherds. "Back, back!" she shouted, thrusting the chair toward the advancing dogs.

George picked up the table lamp and held it out like a club. "Get out of here," she commanded the dogs. "Scram!"

Brutus and Caesar snarled savagely, baring their fangs. Just as the animals seemed about to leap, Professor Herbert entered the office.

"Well, well. If it isn't our nosy little detective and her friend," he said, stepping forward. "I thought I'd seen the last of you two when I forced your car off the road."

"You won't get away with this, Herbert," Nancy said bravely. "We know you switched the real Golden Horse for a fake."

The professor threw back his head and laughed. "So you thought I'd leave it lying around in my office?" he said. "You should give me more credit than that."

"We've already informed the police," Nancy bluffed. "They'll be here any minute."

"Oh, come, come," Herbert mocked. "You can't pull that old gag on me. You and your friend here have been too persistent for your own good. Now I'll have to make sure you keep your cute little noses out of my business once and for all."

George glanced at Nancy, waiting for a signal to spring into action.

Nancy's mind raced as she tried to think of a way to escape. But no one was around, and the dogs were ready to attack on a word from their master.

Herbert marched the girls out of the building and ordered them into the back of his black van, parked near the service entrance.

"Sit down in the corner and don't give me any trouble," he warned them as he tied their hands with cord. Then, motioning to the dogs, he called, "Come on, Brutus, Caesar. Into the van!"

Nancy and George cringed away from the dogs.

"They won't hurt you," Herbert said with a menacing smile, "as long as you don't move." He slammed the van doors closed, then walked around to the front and climbed into the driver's seat.

As the van started off, the dogs settled down on the floor. Nancy started rubbing the cord that bound her wrists against a metal fitting on the side of the van. But Brutus gave a deep-throated growl, forcing her to stop.

"I told you," Herbert called over his shoulder. "Sit still, or the dogs will tear you to pieces."

Nancy caught George's worried look and tried to smile reassuringly.

After a while Nancy could no longer see the streetlights flashing past the tinted windows. It seemed as if they were heading into open country. Then, all at once, the van slowed and turned sharply. After that they climbed a long, steep hillside. The van swayed as it took the hairpin turns of the winding road.

Finally the van reached level ground. Again it slowed, then turned. It bounced down a rutted dirt track, and Nancy could hear bushes scratching against the side of the vehicle as they bumped along.

After a few moments Herbert stopped and turned off the engine. As he climbed out and headed to the back of the van, Nancy whispered to George, "Don't worry, we'll get out of this somehow."

A minute later Herbert pulled open the van door. "Out," he ordered. "And don't try any tricks."

Nancy climbed down from the back, followed by George. In the moonlight she could see a short path leading to a small log cabin ahead.

"Look," Nancy said to Herbert, stalling for time. "Why don't you quit now—before you get in any deeper? Kidnapping is a very serious charge. Margaret Parker has already confessed that she and Stone stole the fake you stuck them with. It's all going to be traced back to you."

"They can't prove anything," Herbert sneered. "And it's too late for you, I'm afraid."

George glared at the professor. "The police will find out that Todd copied the horse for you," she said boldly.

Herbert's eyes widened in surprise. "How did you know that?" he demanded. "Did Todd talk? I'll shut him up, too."

"Then you'll have to kill Fiona Todd as well," Nancy said. "She knows about the copy he made for you."

Herbert blinked. "I'll take care of Fiona."

"And then who will you kill next?" Nancy pressed. "It will never end—until they catch you. And then you'll be sorry you ever got started."

"Enough of your chatter," Herbert ordered, forcing them on. "Move!" He kicked the cabin door open and pushed the girls inside with the dogs close behind them.

Nancy looked around the cabin. Moonlight spilled through the open doorway, shining on the rough-cut floorboards and a small pine table in the center of the room.

Herbert moved the girls over to the far side of the table and started fiddling with a kerosene lantern. A match flared, and Nancy watched as Herbert inserted it into the lamp. A moment later the wick caught, radiating a bright light.

Nancy tensed her muscles, her heart pounding. This was probably her only chance to act.

As Herbert squinted, momentarily blinded by the flame, Nancy took one step forward and kicked the table as hard as she could.

The table toppled over, and the kerosene lantern crashed to the floor. The sound of breaking glass, mingled with Herbert's shrill cry of surprise, startled the dogs. The frightened dogs ran outside yelping.

For a moment the room went dark, then burst into a red flickering glow as the spilled kerosene burst into flames.

Nancy jumped over the fallen table and aimed a karate kick at Herbert. But he was more agile than she had expected. He nimbly stepped aside, and her right foot glanced harmlessly off his hip.

In the next second Nancy felt a stinging blow against her face. She fell backward onto the hard wooden floor, knocking George down with her. Through her blurred vision, Nancy could see the flames beginning to race up the cabin wall.

George scrambled to get up as Nancy tried desperately to free her still-bound hands.

By the light of the raging flames, Nancy saw Herbert leap across the room and kick George aside. Then he stood over Nancy, his chest heaving. A rasping sound came from his throat as his lungs struggled to suck in oxygen amid the thick smoke rising from the fire. His eyes glittered with evil in the firelight. "Why bother putting out the fire?" he wheezed. "I'll just let you burn to death. Such a tragic accident," he mocked as the girls, too, began to cough.

Suddenly Herbert's eyes fell on the jade necklace, now dangling out of Nancy's shirt. In one fluid motion the professor yanked it off her neck. "I'll bet there's a diamond inside!" Herbert exclaimed, staring greedily at the silver locket in his hand. His face contorted in the glare of the flames, and he seemed oblivious to the burning building as he concentrated on forcing the locket open.

Nancy saw her chance and rolled over toward a piece of broken lantern glass. She frantically rubbed the cord binding her wrists against its sharp edge.

Herbert's eyes shone as his fingers pried open the silver lid. Then he sneezed, and a puff of red powder shot into the air. In the next second Herbert screamed in pain. He dropped the necklace and threw his hands up to his face. *"My eyes! They're burning!"* he cried.

Just then Nancy freed her hands and rushed to untie George. Snatching the necklace from the floor, Nancy called to George, "Let's get out of here!"

By now the flames were spreading across the room. The heat had become unbearable, and the girls were coughing heavily from the thick smoke. They darted toward the door as Herbert staggered blindly in circles. As she ran, Nancy put the necklace over her head, relieved that it was safe.

Nancy glanced back at the professor, then grasped George's arm. "We can't leave him here," she said. "He won't be able to find his way out."

George looked up. "The roof's going to fall in soon."

Nancy took a deep breath and dodged back between the flames. She grabbed Herbert by the arm and pushed him toward the door.

Outside, the dogs were circling the burning cabin, snarling and whimpering like wolves. Herbert stumbled out the door and fell to his knees a few yards away.

Nancy and George tried to run toward the van, but the dogs blocked their path, forcing them to halt.

"Get away!" George yelled at the dogs. Then, turning to Nancy, she said, "How do we get out of here before Herbert recovers?"

Just then the flames burst through the roof. The building began to collapse in a shower of sparks, and the dogs suddenly retreated.

"They're afraid of the fire," Nancy said.

"So am I," George retorted.

Nancy picked up a piece of timber, which had fallen near them from the collapsing roof. She charged forward, jabbing the wood in the dogs' snarling faces, until they turned and ran.

Behind them, Nancy heard Herbert crying, *Water! My eyes!*"

Nancy went back and stood over the wailing professor. "I'll give you water," Nancy said, "if you tell us where you've stashed the Golden Horse."

"All right, all right," Herbert said with a moan. "It's buried under a large boulder behind the cabin. Just get me the water before I go blind. There's a jug behind the driver's seat. I keep water in it for the dogs."

Nancy hurried toward the van. A few minutes later Herbert was washing out his eyes with the water.

"I can see," he said, sounding relieved.

Nancy tied the professor's hands tightly behind his back with a dog leash that she'd found in the van. "I'm not sure what was in Su-Lin's locket," she said to George in a low voice, "but it sure smells like cayenne pepper."

A sullen Herbert directed Nancy and George to the spot where he said the Golden Horse was hidden. The girls left him sitting on the ground and then found shovels in a small garden shed near the cabin. Using all their strength, Nancy and George moved the boulder and began to dig in the light of the dying fire.

"I found something!" Nancy cried finally, when her shovel struck something hard. Carefully she unearthed some muddy sacking with something very heavy inside.

She glanced at George, then uncovered the Golden Horse from the sacking. Holding the statue up, she studied it for a long moment. Its smooth, arched back and bridle of rubies glinted in the firelight.

"It's hard to tell the difference between this one and the fake," George said.

"Maybe on the surface," Nancy said. "But the real one has a history that can never be copied. I wonder," she added after a moment, "how many people through the ages have risked everything to possess this magnificent statue?"

It was well past midnight by the time Nancy and George brought Herbert into the Clinton Park police station. The professor was worn and haggard, his face smudged with soot. His eyes, still red and watery from the locket's dust, were now filled with a mixture of fear and anger.

The desk sergeant phoned Lieutenant Higgins at his home, and the lieutenant rushed right over.

"This piece had better be authentic," he said, taking the Golden Horse from Nancy a half hour later. Nancy had already explained Herbert's role in the case, and she now gave the lieutenant the copy of Herbert's letter to Sharp.

Lieutenant Higgins read the letter carefully. "Well, I guess this pretty much clinches Herbert's involvement," he said. "But this Sharp character is real slippery. His name has popped up before in quite a few jewelry thefts. We don't even have a description of the man—and all this letter gives us is a post office address. I doubt if we'll have much luck getting Herbert to talk, at least right now." He flashed Nancy a hopeful smile. "I don't suppose you have any ideas?"

Nancy adjusted her bag on her shoulder as she turned to leave. "Not right now, I'm afraid," she said. "But if I can think of anything, I'll let you know."

"Just a minute," Lieutenant Higgins called. "How

would you feel about taking part in a sting operation —if we can set one up quickly?"

"Sure," Nancy agreed. "I'll do what I can to help."

"We'll figure out something," the lieutenant promised. "We'll work out the details and let you know soon."

Two days later Nancy was briefed on the part she was to play as a police specialist wired her with a tape recorder.

"That looks good," Lieutenant Higgins said finally, inspecting Nancy critically. "Sharp will never suspect a teenager as part of a police sting operation." He sighed. "It's too bad Herbert refused to cooperate. But we're relying on Sharp's greed. He should have already received the forged letter from Herbert that we sent. I have a hunch Sharp will believe Herbert was afraid he was being watched, and that Sharp will agree to pick up the horse from one of Herbert's unsuspecting students."

An hour later Nancy waited at the prearranged meeting place outside the park, carrying the fake statue in a tote bag. She glanced around at the bushes, where she knew the police were hiding, ready to film the exchange on their video cameras. She felt confident that everything was under control. All she had to do now was exchange the statue for the cash.

A few moments later a black Jaguar turned the corner and came racing toward her. It stopped a few feet away. Then a man got out, wearing a tweed suit and a large brimmed hat. He was carrying a leather attaché case. When he looked up, Nancy recognized the blond hair and deep tan.

"Justin Todd," Nancy muttered in disbelief. Todd and Sharp were the same person! Would Todd remember her from the dog show? But before she could shout to the police, Todd rushed forward and grabbed Nancy roughly. Then he hustled her into the car and drove off at high speed!

15

The Chase

Nancy felt a pistol press against her side as Todd steered the speeding car with his left hand.

Swallowing hard, Nancy forced herself to stay calm. "What's going on?" she asked. "I've got some kind of package for you from Professor Herbert." She felt the pressure of the gun ease.

"Herbert would never use Carson Drew's daughter as a go-between," Todd replied. "Who really sent you?"

Nancy wiped her damp palms on her jeans as Todd jumped a red light. Somewhere behind them a police siren began to wail.

"It's the police you're working for, isn't it?" Todd

growled, driving faster. He made a sharp turn through a crowded intersection, narrowly missing another car.

Nancy braced herself against the dashboard as Todd's Jaguar squealed around the turn.

"Tell me!" Todd shouted. "You're working for the police, aren't you?"

"They're traffic cops," Nancy bluffed. "It's your own fault. You jumped that red light back there." She held her breath, hoping he'd believe her.

Suddenly Nancy saw a truck backing out of a side street ahead of them. "Watch out!" she cried. "You'll get us both killed!"

Todd dropped the gun to his lap and drove with both hands, swinging the car around the truck.

Nancy glanced over her shoulder. All she could see was the truck blocking the road. She knew this was Todd's chance to lose the police car.

A few moments later her fears were realized—the police were no longer in sight.

Todd laughed. "Bunch of jerks," he said. "What can you expect from traffic cops?"

Nancy realized she was on her own now. But at least Todd seemed to have bought her story about the police being traffic cops. Her mind raced as she considered her options. Had she convinced him that she was Herbert's go-between, or was Todd still suspicious? She waited for him to make the next move.

Finally Todd said, "I'll soon find out if you're on the level." He turned and glanced at her.

"I don't know what you mean," Nancy said.

Todd reached under the dashboard and pulled out the car phone receiver. Holding it against the steering wheel, he punched in a number. "Give me Professor Herbert," he said into the phone. "No, don't you dare put me on hold!"

"Herbert's not there," Nancy bluffed again. "He's meeting me later to pick up your envelope."

Todd hung up angrily. "I don't believe you."

"Look," Nancy said. "Take my word for it. Professor Herbert asked me to bring your envelope to his cabin later. I've got your package. What more do you want?"

She watched Todd closely. The tension in his face seemed to drain. "Look, I'm tired of this," Nancy went on. "I've been up since five this morning. I had to drive all the way to Herbert's cabin to get this package, whatever it is. Now either you want it, or you don't." She sighed. "All I get out of this is a better grade in my anthropology class."

"All right, all right," Todd said, finally slowing down. "Put the package on the backseat and take the briefcase."

"Briefcase?" Nancy said, trying to sound indignant. "I thought all I had to carry was an envelope."

Todd looked annoyed. "You can tell that fool Herbert that I couldn't fit half a million bucks in an envelope. And—" He stopped suddenly, as if aware that he had said too much.

"Can you drop me back at the park now?" Nancy

145

asked. It was her only chance to draw him back to the police stakeout.

"You can walk," he told her gruffly.

"Not with a case full of cash," Nancy insisted.

Todd made a sharp right and headed back toward the park. He drove at a casual pace, and Nancy relaxed a bit. Todd seemed to trust her now.

Leaning down, Nancy picked up the heavy tote bag and placed it on the backseat. Just then, through the rearview window, she saw a police car making a U-turn. Then it headed toward them, its sirens wailing.

"Oh, no!" she cried. She turned to Todd, as if for help. "What are we going to do?"

Todd muttered angrily to himself, and the car accelerated forward. It swerved across the road, missing an oncoming vehicle by inches. Todd turned into a side street, but two police cars blocked the road. Another police car drew up alongside, forcing the Jaguar onto the curb. Nancy was relieved to see Lieutenant Higgins and his men.

"Get out of the car slowly, with your hands up," the lieutenant said through a megaphone.

Nancy climbed out of the Jaguar, her head still spinning. She leaned against the car while the lieutenant slapped handcuffs on Todd's wrists, reading him his rights.

Justin Todd glared bitterly at Nancy. "I should have known better than to—"

"So, Mr. Sharp," Lieutenant Higgins interrupted.

"I've been waiting to meet you in person for some time."

"His real name is Justin Todd," Nancy told the officer. "He's the jeweler who made the fake for Herbert." Running her fingers through her hair, Nancy added, "You might also want to check out his wife, Fiona."

"Keep Fiona out of this!" Justin Todd snarled. "She had nothing to do with it."

"Why did you do it?" she asked.

"The same reason Herbert did," he said. "Money, what else?"

"Sounds as if you'll have plenty to talk about with the professor in jail," Lieutenant Higgins said, pushing Todd into the backseat of the police car. Then the lieutenant turned to Nancy and smiled. "Well done, Nancy Drew. Maybe we can work together again sometime."

A few days later Nancy was invited to attend a celebration at the Clinton Park Museum with her father and friends.

"So how does it feel to receive a medal of honor from the Clinton Park police?" Bess asked, when Nancy returned from the podium.

Nancy gave her friends a hug. "As I said in my speech, this medal belongs to you and George, too. I couldn't have pulled it off without you guys. Thanks."

"Anytime," George said with a grin.

Su-Lin leaned across the table. "Congratulations,

Nancy," she said. "It's so nice to have the Golden Horse back in the museum. I'll never be able to thank you enough for helping me and my father."

"Yes, Nancy," Lee Tung added. "We thank you from the bottom of our hearts."

Nancy smiled. "Oh, I almost forgot," she said, turning to Su-Lin. "Your necklace really did protect me, after all." Nancy reached into her bag and pulled out a small box. "Thanks again for loaning this to me. But I'm afraid all the red powder that was inside the locket is gone."

Su-Lin giggled. "You mean the cayenne pepper. George just told me how it got into Professor Herbert's eyes."

Nancy turned and saw Officer Jenkins approaching their table.

"Hi, Nancy," he said, then nodded to her friends. "Lieutenant Higgins asked me to tell you that Professor Herbert has finally made a full confession. You and your friend did a great job rounding him up."

"Thanks," Nancy said. "By the way, I meant to ask you—did Professor Herbert know that Sharp was really Justin Todd?"

Officer Jenkins nodded. "Herbert knew it all along. But it seems that Todd's wife, Fiona, had no idea what was going on. All she knew was that her husband had made a copy of the Golden Horse for the professor."

"What about Nelson Stone?" Nancy asked.

"Lieutenant Higgins put him through some rough questioning," the officer told her. "Stone finally broke down and confessed. His story jibes with Margaret Parker's. They're both being charged with theft and attempted fraud. Stone's prints match the ones left on the knife that you found in your car."

George leaned forward. "What was Professor Herbert charged with?" she asked.

"Oh, theft, kidnapping, and attempted murder," Jenkins replied.

"What about Todd?" Bess piped up. "Nancy said you guys have been after him for a long time."

"We certainly have," the officer agreed. "He's been charged with a very long list of crimes."

"Excuse me," Nancy said, standing up. "But I'd like to go over and congratulate Hillary Lane."

"What for?" Bess asked.

"Didn't you hear?" George whispered. "She's been appointed the new curator of the Clinton Park Museum."

"And she's even donated her Golden Horse to the Tibetan collection," Nancy added. "Isn't that wonderful? They'll make an announcement later in the evening."

"Just think," Bess mused. "After all these years the pair of statues will finally be together."

A few feet away, the heiress was talking to Carson Drew. The girls couldn't help overhearing her say, "I always knew Aunt Amanda did the right thing when she donated her estate for the museum."

Bess nudged Nancy. "Did you hear *that?*" she whispered.

149

"I guess she's singing a different tune, now that she's the new curator," George said, chuckling.

"Well, at least the story has a happy ending," Nancy said.

Su-Lin smiled brightly. "And it's all thanks to Nancy Drew."

NANCY DREW® MYSTERY STORIES By Carolyn Keene

THE HARDY BOYS® SERIES By Franklin W. Dixon